The Surrency Affair

Louis Berry

Dear Reader,

Your time and heart invested in my stories mean the world to me. I pour my soul into crafting each novel, driven by a relentless work ethic to ensure your enjoyment shines through every page. As a solitary writer, I humbly ask you to share my work with friends who love a good tale. Your recommendation fuels my journey, and I'm endlessly grateful for your support.

With sincerest appreciation,

Louis

Discover other titles as well as upcoming releases from Louis Berry at:
www.louisberryauthor.com

1

The Fruit Growers Express began operations on March 18, 1920, in Jacksonville, Florida. A row of warehouses contained within a single building situated alongside rail tracks provided incredible logistical efficiency for the times. Men labored, loading, and unloading refrigerated boxcars. Fruit grown in Florida was shipped all over the nation from the location. Bib overalls and work boots were the uniform for those needing protection from wooden fruit crates containing shiv-like splinters.

Atlantic Coast Line Railroad established the hub in Jacksonville that brought opportunity to an otherwise depressed community. Its influence would be felt until 1986 when purchased by CSX Transportation. The area thrived for decades, but 1936 still proved a struggle for those incapable of employing requisite foresight to see good times ahead.

It had been three years since Roosevelt outlawed private ownership of gold, making physical dollars the only representation of wealth with properties that stimulated tactile senses of security. Those who'd trusted banks lost all in the 1929 stock market crash. By 1936, resilient ones reached a point of recovery through brute strength.

Criminals suffered due to the repeal of prohibition in 1933. Illegal spirits provided men who flaunted the law a means by which to amass wealth. Lucrative revenue streams disappeared, and the void required filling.

Occupying one end of the warehouse complex was a small lunch counter operated by John and Mayme Surrency. The couple had been married for thirty years. John was ten years his wife's senior and possessed the strength of Joab. He witnessed the struggles that possessed his wife. Resolute was the man to do everything possible to provide her happiness.

Years earlier Mayme had a hysterectomy. Post operation therapy included morphine, to which she became addicted. John witnessed his once stunning wife as she withered beneath external influences. Fleeting blame was rationalized as nothing more than an aging visage. Employed intellect stoked awareness that drugs exacerbated his wife's decline. It pained him, but he resolved to stand by the commitment he'd made on their wedding day.

November 25, 1936, was the day before Thanksgiving. There was an air of happiness along the warehouse platform. Men busied about their day, looking forward to spending time with extended family for the holiday. In addition to food service, John and Mayme were allowed by the owner of the lunch counter to operate a check cashing business for the workers. Weekly paychecks were normally cashed on Fridays. The holiday pressed the couple to provide not only food and cash, but for Mayme to help with Thanksgiving preparations.

The couple's daughter Miriam hosted Thanksgiving in her Arlington home on Windermere Drive. The daughter was married to Noble Enge, a man of Norwegian descent. His parents lived next door and were always included in festivities. Miriam's father-in-law, Nils Enge, was a stoic man who wore a long gray beard. During most family occasions he could be seen wearing a black suit, with gray shirt and tie and a black cowboy hat.

Noble had two brothers. The three operated a successful graphic design studio on East Forsyth. During a time of black and white print, the brothers brought color into the fledgling graphic design profession.

Miriam's home was plenty large to host everyone. A large lot covered the length of the block, offering room for relatives to mingle outside during cool fall afternoons. Her

2

youngest sister and family would be there. She was also called Mayme. Everyone called her Baby.

Most days John and Mayme spent together operating the food concession and doing that which was necessary to make a living during economically depressed times. The day before Thanksgiving offered the opportunity for Mayme to gather provisions and make the trek to Arlington and Miriam's house to help set up for the following day. Her daughter had three young children. Theodore Noble, Junior, who everyone referred to as Ted, was nearly eight years old. Polio rendered the boy's left leg nearly useless, and the only thing that gave his body support was a metal brace wrapped by leather straps. Bess was nearly six years old, and Carol nearly three. Baby and her two-year-old son were at Aunt Miriam's house. The children loved when their grandmother came for a visit. Anticipation on that day was palpable.

John knew time with family would be good for his wife. There was purpose in her matriarchy. The man understood love conquered all and possessed the power to eradicate her demons. John stood atop the elevated platform, wearing a soiled apron, and waved goodbye to his wife as she set off on errands, and then to their daughter's home.

Mayme drove from work over the Saint Johns River Bridge into San Marco. Although she preferred the personal attention of her grocer in Springfield, time was of the essence.

Excitement abounded as the woman filled her car with items she and John could contribute to a bountiful Thanksgiving for children and grandchildren. Times had been hard for so long, and the proverbial light at the end of the tunnel was coming into view. Anticipation of the joy experienced with family pushed any thought of morphine from the woman's consciousness. Visions of grandchildren's cherub-like faces drew back the corners of her mouth and manifested a grin felt genuinely within her soul. For all of her troubles, Mayme understood her daughters, and grandchildren, represented her thriving contribution to the human race. Evil's grip might not loosen control upon her, but her family was alive, well, and most importantly, happy.

Mayme's circuitous route took her from San Marco east on Highway 90, and then to Chaseville Road south for a quarter mile, and then onto the northern section of the road. Once over the Chaseville Bridge, she maneuvered the ninety-degree curve that set her path straight to Windermere Drive. Better economic times afforded her and John the opportunity to purchase a new 1936 Ford 4 door Sedan. In the backseat was a fresh turkey, a bag of cranberries for sauce, and two fresh loaves of bread: one to be used for dressing. Flour and eggs provided the raw materials for rolls and pie crusts. Mayme's heart was full.

Two-year-old Carol was the first grandchild to meet Mayme at her car upon arrival. There was purpose on the toddler's face as she walked quickly on unsteady legs to the driver's door. She held her tiny hands fist-like, as if pulling herself closer to her grandmother. Taking caution to not knock her granddaughter over, the old woman opened the door slowly. Once the little countenance appeared in the gap, she picked her from the ground and quickly placed the little girl in her lap. Carol babbled incessantly sharing all of her new words with her grandmother.

Moments later she looked to see Bess and Ted emerge from the house. The two, more mature children, approached the car in a more controlled manner. Ted moved almost business-like, dragging his left leg along with him.

After all requisite hugs were given, Mayme looked up to see her daughter standing in the doorway, holding the screen door open and standing in its gap. "Do you need any help?" she called to her mother.

"I think Ted and I can handle it."

"Okay," Miriam replied before disappearing inside the house.

After Ted gave a muted hug with one arm and leaned in with his shoulder, he opened the back door of the car and grabbed bags for the trek inside.

"I'll get the eggs, Ted." It was the day before Thanksgiving. Grocers would have run out of fresh eggs. She didn't wish to risk their celebration on a mishap.

Mayme walked slowly down the sidewalk holding the tray of eggs as Bess and Carol danced about her legs like gnats vying for attention. She walked all the way inside the house, through the living room and into the kitchen at the rear of the home. Placing the eggs on the table, she then reached with her free hands and embraced both girls. She pressed them into her legs with a hand on each girl's back. Boundless affection was returned by each granddaughter squeezing Mayme's legs as tightly as little arms allowed.

Without noticing, Miriam walked into the kitchen and alerted her mother to the first Thanksgiving tragedy. "Baby dropped the pumpkin pies on the floor. We have no pie for Thanksgiving."

Mayme shot a quick look at her daughter. From inside the living room, she heard her youngest daughter's voice. "Mama, I didn't drop them. I put them on the washing machine to cool and decided to get some laundry done. The shaking of the machine pushed them right off onto the floor. It's not my fault," she proclaimed, as tears welled in her eyes. "I swear my life is like the dark hinges of hell."

"Don't worry, Baby. I can run by the farmer's market and get another pumpkin. I'll make the pie tonight at home and bring it in the morning." Mayme reassured her daughter everything was going to be alright.

With granddaughters still attached to her legs, Mayme leaned into a hug with Miriam and then Baby, who'd entered the room. "I've got to go pick up your father at the bank and get him back to the lunch counter to cash the guys' checks."

"Okay, mama," both women replied, before Baby offered a bit of advice. "You drive that fancy new Ford safely, okay?"

"I will," Mayme responded before turning to leave the house.

As she entered the living room at the front of the home, she saw Ted had taken up a seat next to his Norwegian grandfather. "Bye, Ted." She shifted her gaze to the old, bearded man who spoke little English. Feeling the need to speak loudly so the man could understand her, Mayme called to the old man, "I'll see you tomorrow, Mr. Enge."

The old man responded with a wave of his hand as he sat with a crossword puzzle in his lap, and a pencil in his hand. Miriam helped her father-in-law with the game as a means of learning English.

Mayme exited the house, walked down the sidewalk, and loaded into her new Ford. Although John waited for her at the bank just across the river, the fact that Jacksonville only had one bridge made the route time consuming. She glanced at the underside of her left wrist where she kept her watch. Making John wait wasn't top of mind, it was the men who worked at the Fruit Growers Express who counted on them to cash checks. She raced to get there before the 12:30 lunch break ended.

As she approached Barnett Bank, she saw her husband standing outside talking with the bank president. Maneuvering the car into an empty space in front of the men, she waved.

The president returned the gesture. He knew time was short and they needed to get back to the warehouse.

Mayme slid across the front seat, allowing her husband to drive them back to work. They exchanged a pleasant kiss before John turned and looked over his right shoulder while backing out of the space. "Did everything go okay at Miriam's?"

"Perfectly. Well, except for Baby."

The man looked at his wife. "What did she do now?"

His wife smiled. "She placed the pumpkin pies on the washing machine in order for them to cool, and then did a load of laundry. The vibration of the machine sent the pies onto the floor." She paused. "Oh, and we need to stop and get a pumpkin on the way home."

John leaned toward his wife, turned the steering wheel in the same direction using the hand-over-hand technique and smiled. "Sometimes I think that girl is cursed," and then chuckled.

The couple retraced a path they'd driven hundreds of times over their seventeen years at the Grower's Express. As the man straightened the vehicle's path on Kings Road, he noticed a car blocking the street ahead. He slowed the vehicle's speed and came to a stop yards from the car. Inside he saw two, young, black men. "I'll see if they need help," John told his wife.

Inside the supposedly stalled car were Alvin Tyler and James Baker, the latter drove the car. Between them was a .45 caliber pistol. Intent on robbing the couple, the men had been told John would be carrying at least two hundred dollars. Baker's nerves got the better of him and pleaded with his acquaintance to not go through with it. "Let me just drive away. We can't do this."

Tyler barked his response as he reached for the gun between the two. "I'll take care of this. They say this man is a scared man. He'll be easy to rob."

"Don't do it, man." Baker pled.

His accomplice sat silently holding the gun in his lap.

John approached the car with a smile. "You fellas need some help?"

Without conscience, Tyler stepped out of the car and approached Mr. Surrency. When the men were close enough to shake hands, the young man brandished the gun which he'd been holding behind his back. Without thought, John lunged at the man and began punching him. A cut opened on the left eye of the young man, who pushed toward his victim. When his momentum carried John to the ground, the young man swung the butt of his gun toward the man's head. Defensively, the old man was able to grab the wrist of his assailant just enough to slow its progress. Nevertheless, a blow was struck that stung the old man. Feeling at a disadvantage Surrency gathered himself and crawled, before standing, and hurrying back to his car. There he had a weapon of his own.

The old man felt nervously under the driver's seat until he sensed the familiar form of his .38 caliber weapon. Tyler chased after him. John fell into his seat and faced the assailant as he approached.

Baker emerged from the assailant's car in order to retrieve his accomplice and leave before things got worse. Mayme saw the second man approaching to seemingly assault her husband. She got out of the car, made her way around the front, and began pulling Baker away from the altercation.

Before John was able to aim and fire, Tyler unloaded five bullets into the man's chest and torso. Mayme and Baker heard the gunfire and turned to witness the murder. The woman saw her husband bleeding profusely from several wounds. Stepping back away from the scene, Mayme stumbled and fell into the roadside ditch. Without remorse, Tyler walked around the front of the car while reloading his pistol. He faced the fifty-three-year-old woman. She looked at him stoically, unafraid of what was to come. The robber turned murderer raised his gun and shot twice. The first bullet pierced her abdomen and lodged next to her spine. The second missed her body but was caught in the fabric of her dress.

As the reality of the carnage set into the psyches of the young men, they quickly ran back to their car. Once inside, they drove speedily, but only to the end of the road. Slamming on the brakes and becoming engulfed in a cloud of dust from the dirt road. The two men bounced out of their car and ran toward an open field. Jumping the fence, they scurried across the pasture. Baker possessed more speed and easily beat the assassin to an awaiting getaway car on the far side of the field.

Tyler made it to the car and found his accomplice lying on the floor of the backseat. A white man was driving and implored the second assailant to get in so they could leave the crime scene. The second man jumped across the backseat and lay flat. The driver sped away and the back door slammed shut under the influence of the undulating car that swerved along the dirt road.

When the trio felt safely away from the scene, the two men sat up in the back seat. Tyler admitted to the driver, "you said that man was a scared man. He's got more guts than any man I ever see'd. You know I had to shoot him. I think I killed him."

Seemingly without concern for their lost loot, the driver replied, "what of it; let the motherfucker die."

2

The Office of the State's Attorney for the Fourth District was abuzz concerning Wednesday's murder. Mayme clung to life. It was the day after Thanksgiving. Garland Headley headed the office. He'd held the position of lead prosecutor for nearly five years. Having worked his way up through the State's Attorney's office, he'd proven himself as fair and balanced. At a time when local elites attempted to wrest control of resources from those deemed unworthy, the idealist lawyer applied legal concepts on an even keel. Adversaries still embraced the outdated concept of frontier justice and spoke of the need to rid the town of the man's presence in order to advance agendas.

Typewriter strikers could be heard rhythmically hitting rollers advancing paper throughout the open floor plan of the outer office. Garland strode through the activity of assistants and secretaries on the way to his office. In his hand were current copies of both local newspapers, The Florida Times Union, and the Jacksonville Journal.

Stopping at the door to his office, Garland removed his key ring from his pocket and unlocked the door. He walked inside, closing the door behind him. Tossing the newspapers onto his desk, he walked to the rear corner of the room, removed his suit jacket, and hung it on a coat tree. The man wore pleated pants, a smartly pressed white shirt, and suspenders. The office was enclosed by the same limestone walls as the exterior of the building. It offered the utmost in privacy for a man who carried on meetings on behalf of the county. Near the room's exterior wall was a large, functional, fireplace that spoke to the opulence offered those who held the position.

The man made his way to his chair, sat down, and reclined after retrieving the top newspaper from his desk. 'Bandits Slay J.H. Surrency; Wound Wife,' was the headline that caught his attention. It would be up to his office to prosecute the perpetrators. He read the article with great interest.

Upon reading the name of the female victim, Garland's brow furrowed with recognition. He read it aloud for confirmation. "Mayme Swearingen Surrency."

Garland tossed the paper onto the desk as he leaned forward. He reached over and held down the intercom button and beckoned his secretary to complete the task. "Miss Goldman, can you please have Oliver Morris meet me in my office?"

"Yes, sir," came a quick reply.

Garland retrieved the paper once again and read the article three times before his assistant state attorney made it into the room. The men worked side-by-side for over a decade and the need for formality had long been cast aside. Oliver entered the room and took the familiar seat in front of the man's desk.

Garland looked at his friend and associate, tilted his head, and asked, "does the name Swearingen mean anything to you?"

The man leaned back in his chair and scratched his scalp at the point of his receding hairline. "God, yes, but I can't place it. Did we go to law school with a Swearingen?"

Garland wagged his finger at the answer, as if trying to keep a thought aloft in his consciousness. "I don't think we did, but it's an oddly familiar name."

The men sat in silence, contemplating the significance of a name that surfaced as a result of a local murder. Garland stared through his office window, onto Monroe Street, as if an anthropomorphized epiphany would appear from the sunlight's glare.

Garland sat forward sharply, and once again beckoned his secretary, "Miss Goldman, can you please get the State's Attorney in Bartow on the line for me?"

"Yes, sir."

He smiled at the associate seated across from him. "There was a state senator killed in a car wreck with that last name."

Oliver nodded.

"Mr. Headley, Mr. Judd is on the line for you."

Without a word in response, Garland quickly lifted the phone's receiver from its cradle. "Grady. How have you been?" He paused as he listened to the man's response. "Heather and kids doing well, I hope?"

After the pleasantries had been dispensed on part of both men, Garland asked the question that bothered him since reading the name in the paper. "Does the name Swearingen mean anything to you?"

Oliver watched the smile grow on his boss' face. Garland looked at his associate and nodded through his grin. The attorney listened intently. The story was long and filled with details. As the man signed off, he suggested, "listen, the Tars are playing baseball again. If you get up this way next season, we can take in a game. We could do some deep-sea fishing too." He paused, listening to the response. "Okay, you take care, too." He replaced the phone on its cradle.

"Have you seen the paper today?"

"Not yet," Oliver responded.

"There was a man murdered and his wife shot yesterday over by the Fruit Growers Express. Her maiden name is Swearingen. Well, in 1931 there was a state senator named Swearingen killed in a car wreck. That incident stuck in my memory because the state attorney down there always said there was something fishy about the crash. He just confirmed that."

Ever the skeptic, Oliver argued, "maybe it's simply a coincidence?"

Garland shrugged. "Maybe, but I'm going to the hospital to find out if they're related."

Oliver smiled, knowing that whenever his boss latched onto something, he was like a dog on a bone. "Don't forget to pack your decorum."

Garland chuckled. "I won't."

3

Mayme had been rushed to County Hospital. It was the facility designated to receive only indigent patients; those unable to pay for medical care.

John and his wife established themselves in Bartow as a young family with four children. After the youngest girl, named for her mother, was born the mother found herself in need of a hysterectomy. Weeks at Johns Hopkins relieved the woman of her uterus but bestowed a dependency to Morphine. Upon returning to Bartow, she found her local doctor more than willing to feed her addiction.

With financial backing from his brother Winder Surrency, John established an experimental citrus grove in Polk County. His brother was a well-respected attorney in Sarasota who dabbled in the political realm.

The father of four witnessed the continued decline of his wife for several years. She sold the family silver and any other item of value her husband wouldn't immediately miss to feed a growing dependency on drugs. Separate existences eventually collided, and John was devastated to learn the magnitude of his wife's addiction. Markers had been settled and assets liquidated in order to clear her debt. The man's love for his wife never wavered.

Losing everything in Bartow facilitated the move to Jacksonville in 1917. The town possessed an economy that thrived and offered opportunity. The hamlet's population was a mere fifty-two thousand. In the twenty-five years subsequent, there grew to be three times as many residents. In 1936 the city owned more municipal utility companies than any city in the world. Without motive for profit, rates were kept low, and citizens benefitted. The burgeoning railroad system provided for John and Mayme. Jacksonville offered an environment whereby the family could thrive.

The couple worked shoulder to shoulder for that time, and John's strength of character supported his wife and she slowly matured beyond her dependence on morphine. A love could not have grown stronger between man and wife. Although Mayme had grown beyond feeding her addiction, its specter remained.

Albeit successful, the couple hadn't nearly reached the point of wealth that afforded the finer things in life as experienced in Bartow. Four young children sapped resources until the point they'd grown and started lives of their own. It was then John and Mayme accumulated that which would provide during their golden years. It was still not enough to avoid rushing Mayme to the County Hospital in Jacksonville to treat her gunshot wounds. The infirmary was located at the corner of Jessie and Franklin Streets. It was thitherward Garland Headley hoped to find a recovering victim of senseless violence.

The tall, handsome state's attorney strode the corridor of the hospital confidently as he worked his way toward Mayme's room. He'd received word late on the night of Thanksgiving the victim's condition had improved. Good news offered hope. Although it was his job to prosecute crimes, the opportunity for one less murder conviction was welcomed.

His pace slowed as he approached room 117. Nearing his destination, burgeoning reticence hindered progress toward a favored outcome. Emerging from the doorway of Mayme's room was her second daughter, Bess. Her countenance was sullen, and tear soaked. Garland stopped, not wishing to present an overbearing presence. He painted a half-smile on his face, offering familiarity with the young woman's situation.

Bess walked past the attorney without lifting her gaze from the floor. "Miss Surrency?"

The woman stopped and turned to look back at the man. "Mrs. DeVaughn."

"My apologies." The man held his hat in hand by its brim and bowed his head slightly asking forgiveness. "Are you Mrs. Surrency's daughter?"

The woman nodded.

The man ever-so-gently extended his hand in friendship. "My name is Garland Headley. I'm the state's attorney who will be trying the murder case of your father."

Glibly, the woman responded, "add another murder trial to your docket."

The man's face fell. He'd gotten a report the prior evening that Mayme was improving, and she had been strong enough to give detectives a description of the men who'd attempted to rob them. "I'm sorry. I heard she was doing well last night."

"She died at four A.M."

"I am so sorry. Please accept my condolences."

"You're very kind, Mr. Headley." The woman turned and began to walk away.

"Mrs. DeVaughn," he called after her.

She stopped, turned, and mustered an inquisitive smile; willing to accept whatever the man had to say.

For a man who'd never entered a courtroom unprepared, he found himself grasping for the right words to say. Nothing about this family who'd suffered such a violent tragedy ever entered his consciousness. Although he aspired to higher political office, motives were genuine. "I'm sorry."

"You said that before."

"Yeah, but I'm now sorry you've been made to suffer for your mother."

"Suffering's all the same, Mr. Headley."

The man closed his eyes and shook his head at his frustration permeating Bess' state of mind. "I'm actually a lot more intelligent than I sound."

"God, I hope so, if you're the one trying the case." She paused. "Is there anything else?"

"Please forgive my stammering. When I was told your mother was improving last night, I became hopeful. I've just been gut-punched."

"Imagine how I feel."

Garland nodded. "There's something about this case that screams some other motive. Investigators haven't had a chance to do their jobs, but at first blush, something seems rotten in the state of Denmark." He shook his head. "I can comprehend and try a case whereby two troglodyte dock workers get into a fight; one pulls a knife and kills the other. It's easily dismissed. I can't dismiss this case so easily. A husband and wife so obviously targeted?" He shook his head, again. "Not buying the fact it was a robbery gone wrong."

Bess turned, and fully faced the attorney. "Mr. Headley …"

"Please call me Garland."

"Garland … My mother was not without faults, but I will love her unconditionally and eternally. Nothing will ever change that. Father was a strong man, and he loved my mother so absolutely that I know they are together as we speak. He fought to keep men away that meant her harm. No longer does he need to fight for her. Now they can simply exist together. I take solace in that." She shrugged her shoulders. "What's done is done."

Garland shook his head vigorously. "No. I won't accept that. The sheriff will find who perpetrated this crime, and I will personally make them pay."

Bess smiled genuinely at the man who embraced the well-being of her family. "Mr. … Garland, we had nothing to celebrate yesterday. Thanksgiving was always our favorite holiday. I'm afraid that is no more. However, my siblings and I are gathering at my sister's house tomorrow to partake in all we'd planned for yesterday. You're welcome to join us. Bring your wife and kids."

17

"I'm not married."

"So be it. The house is on Windermere Drive in Arlington."

Headley nodded affirmation of his familiarity with the area. When he didn't respond verbally, Bess turned and began to walk down the corridor.

Recalling his conversation that morning with Oliver Morris, he called to the woman. "One more thing. Was your mother related to the Swearingen who was the state senator from Bartow killed in a car accident in 1931?"

The woman stopped, turned, and nodded. "He was our uncle ... my mother's brother."

4

Miriam and Noble Enge's house sat on a lot that encompassed the block's depth from Windermere Drive to Wiltshire Street. Garland arrived and saw several cars parked bumper-to-bumper in the driveway. He drove to the cross street, Almira, turned left and then backed onto Windermere before pulling his car along the edge of the front yard.

The day was cool and without humidity. It was the time of year people flocked to Florida to avoid harsh winters in their home state. Garland approached the screen door and rapped on its wooden frame. There was no answer, but he heard voices. He adjusted his head to offer an angle to peer through the living room and kitchen. A sliver of window that opened onto the backyard could be seen. Several people sat at a picnic table. The state's attorney stood back and looked at the door. Deciding it best to trespass from the side yard rather than through the house, he walked down the path, under the trees, and around the corner of the house.

As he manipulated the chain-link gate, he suddenly considered the possibility of being met by an unruly dog. He looked at the bottle of red wine in his hand as his only means of self-defense. Shaking away his fear as irrational, Garland continued around the side of the house.

Eclipsing its corner, he watched as several people on the far side of the picnic table recognized a stranger entered their property. Miriam, Noble, Jack, and Sarah each took notice of Garland as he walked. There seemed to be nothing threatening about a man dressed in a suit and carrying an unopened bottle of wine. The situation seemed all too normal for a family in mourning. The state's attorney watched as Miriam leaned across the table toward her younger sister, whose back was to the man who approached. Bess turned and recognized Garland.

The woman stood quickly and walked to the man. "Thank you for coming by. Here, I'll introduce you to everyone." Everyone seated with their back to Garland pivoted and straddled the bench beneath them, and then looked at the man. Bess motioned over their heads and began on the far side of the table, from left to right. "This is my sister Miriam, and her husband Noble. This is their house. My brother Jack and his girlfriend Sarah." She shifted their focus on those who sat on the near side of the table. "This is my husband, Shannon. Next, we have Ed, who is Baby's husband, and finally we have Baby." She paused, thinking of her mother. Tears gathered at her bottom eyelid. "Baby's given name is Mayme. We've just always referred to her as Baby."

Garland bowed slightly. "It's nice to meet you all. Please accept my condolences." He held the bottle of wine forward before leaning toward and placing it on the table. "I brought this for dinner."

Bess, Shannon, Ed, and Baby all scooted to the left on their bench to afford room for Garland to take a seat.

The second sibling filled the others in on Garland's purpose in entering their lives. "For those of you who don't pay attention to local politics, Mr. Headley is our esteemed State's Attorney. He came by the hospital yesterday to visit mother."

Nods of understanding were offered by all, except Baby. She appeared to not be engaged in the conversation. Garland found her energy disquieting.

Miriam picked up on their visitor's discomfort from across the table and offered an interrogatory designed to place the man at ease. "Mr. Headley, have you had a chance to speak with the sheriff?"

Gladly, he engaged the woman at the far end of the table. "Yes, and I'm happy to say the investigation is progressing nicely."

"Anything you can tell us?"

The man shook his head. "No. I really can't speak to the investigation. I can tell you there are several leads and eyewitnesses who've come forward. It seems your parents were well-liked around the Fruit Growers Express."

"That's nice," Miriam concluded.

Assessing whether it was the right time to inquire, Garland charged forth and asked, "can you tell me a little about your parents?"

In unison, the in-laws sat backward, yielding to spouses. All of whom leaned forward into the table and gazed at the attorney, except Baby. She remained distant. Bess felt compelled to speak first. "I told Mr. Headley that mother had her issues, and that father loved and fought for her."

"There was a boy who told Mama he could get her morphine pills and father beat the boy and told him to stay away," Jack offered.

"Stop lyin', Jack," Miriam implored.

"I am not lying, Sister. Father told me about it. He also said the boy tried to get Mama hooked on heroin, but she couldn't accept the needle."

"Jack," Bess interjected. "I'm not sure Mr. Headley needs to witness our dirty laundry."

Jack shook his head. "I'm sure Mr. Headley knows a lot more than we do, and he probably already knows about mama's issues."

Garland glanced at all of the faces that stared directly at him. "First of all, please call me Garland. Secondly, regardless of your mother's issues, she's going to get justice ... as will your father."

Suddenly, a cool breeze rustled the leaves in the trees. It was devoid of the humidity suffered during summer months in

Florida. For the first time Baby spoke. "Feel that velvet breeze. Mama loved this time of year."

Garland attempted to capture the youngest daughter's attention while she appeared lucid. "Did your mother enjoy Thanksgiving?"

For the first time the girl engaged their guest. She turned and smiled at the man. "It was her favorite holiday."

Once the visitor experienced her soul manifested, he enjoyed what a stunning young lady she was. Benevolence motivated him to engage her further. "How did you and Ed meet?"

Slipping back into her catatonic state, she merely offered a "Hmm," and a shrug of her shoulders.

Ed spoke up. "You remember, Baby." He turned his attention to the attorney. "We were at the Ocean View Pavilion at Jacksonville Beach. Baby loves riding the roller coaster. Anyway, we were both inside the pavilion. I noticed her at a perfume counter. I thought she was so pretty, and I went up to ask her name."

Garland smiled at the recollection. He glanced at Baby, who maintained a muted smile, and then back to Ed.

"When I did, she turned and sprayed me with one of those perfume atomizers. Right in the face. That's when I knew she was the girl for me."

The visitor furrowed his brow, not understanding affection as witnessed by Ed.

Baby's husband laughed and shook his head. "I had that bitter taste in my mouth all night."

Miriam looked at Garland. "Mayme's a bit cosseted. Once you get past that, you'll understand she really is a wonderful girl."

Bess leaned into the table to look their visitor in the eye. He mimicked her move and the two gazed at one another. "This has hit her the hardest. You'll have to forgive Baby."

"Maybe if you didn't refer to her as Baby," Garland thought to himself. "It's okay."

Suddenly, a flock of kids led by Ted Enge approached the table from the rear of the yard. Included was five-year-old, Bess, two-year-old Carol, and Phillip Slater, Baby and Ed's son. The group came from the chicken enclosure at the rear of the property. "When are we gonna eat?" Ted asked.

His father Noble replied, "In about an hour. The adults are visiting."

Miriam noticed the brace on her son's left leg was stretched beyond capacity. She leaned toward her husband. "Noble, we really need to get Ted a new brace. He's growing out of that one."

The man nodded and responded in his Norwegian laden accent. "I'll take him to Bremer Brace next week and get him fitted."

Another cool breeze blew through the yard. Without a word, Baby shivered exaggeratedly for all to notice.

Garland listened to the group as they fondly recalled the idiosyncrasies their mother displayed throughout her life. The attorney appreciated the opportunity to get to know the family for whom he'd fight to ensure murderers were brought to justice.

A commotion from deep within the property drew the man's focus away from the conversation. The kids were making noise. Garland watched intently while still listening to the conversation. It appeared the little girl Bess was goading her brother into something. What it was the man couldn't hear. Curiously, he watched as Ted flung his dead leg away from its strong counterpart. The boy leaned over and placed his right palm onto the ground. Using that arm and his good leg, the boy walked around the yard as normally as those with two good legs. "That young man is going places," the attorney thought to himself.

Ted's heroics further solidified Garland's belief there was something special about this family. He turned away from the kids and dipped back into adult conversation.

5

The last day of November 1936 was a Monday and found Garland Headley in his office. It was an especially cold day and he'd built a fire in his office fireplace. He stood and walked around his desk, across the room, and stopped at the hearth. He grabbed the poker from its rack and pushed the logs around to intensify heat. Cold air drafted in from single pane windows, consuming the heat as it ventured father from its source. Caulking between the frame and glass proved insufficient to keep winter winds at bay. Garland stood still to bask in the benefit of heat generated from the fire. He turned in place and looked at the stack of files on his desk. Most were thick with arrest and court documents. One, especially thin, represented the murder of John and Mayme Surrency. At thirty-five years of age, he'd seen a lot of criminal activity. Acts of violence had always been viewed by the prosecutor as an almost neanderthal reaction; something buried deeply within humans only few allowed to get the better of them. He'd gladly sent men to jail who possessed creative talents the world never witnessed. Those possessing the artistic ability to express in great detail the beauty contained in nature yet were consumed by ever-present violent embers that lurched forth upon provocation. It was then criminals lost connection to a world that flourished beyond their earthly existence.

Of all the paperwork on his desk, it was the singular thin file that commanded Garland's attention. Its only contents were the initial police report. As evidence continued to be gathered the file would grow, until its eventual disposition among successful convictions his office garnered. It was the fact John and Mayme Surrency did nothing to spark hatred within a living soul that perplexed the man. Words were tossed about to the point of commonality. Dilution caused them to lose their meaning. Senseless was just such a word. Nonetheless, it was the only word that occupied the mind of the educated man, as he stared across his office at the skinny file.

The voice of Garland's secretary sparked from the intercom speaker on his desk. "Sheriff Swift is here to see you."

"Send him in," he yelled toward the door to his office. "Dammit," he exclaimed as he was forced to move away from the fire and answer directly. He stood at his desk, leaned toward its business side, and pressed down the switch to activate the mechanism. "Send him in." Quickly, the attorney made his way back toward the warmth of the fire.

When the sheriff breached his doorway, Garland called to the man. "Let's meet over here by the fire. This cold air has me chilled to the bone."

The sheriff walked over without a word, placed the file he carried on the coffee table situated between two sofas placed perpendicularly to the fireplace. He stood next to the prosecutor and warmed his hands over the fire.

"How many cases do you have for us to go over today?" the prosecutor asked.

The sheriff offered one quick shake of his head. "Only one."

The attorney glanced at the size of the file on the table. "That's a lot of paperwork for one case."

"It's the Surrency case."

"And?"

"My deputies are working overtime on this one. Some have even volunteered to sacrifice vacation days to catch these guys."

Garland walked toward his desk and called back to the sheriff, "Open the file and show me what you've got." He stopped and retrieved a cigarette box and stick lighter from his desk. Walking back to the coffee table, he set the items next to the open file the sheriff displayed on its surface. "Would you like a cigarette?"

"No thank you."

The prosecutor shook his head. "I don't smoke a lot, but it keeps me warm on days like this." The man opened the cigarette box, retrieved one, and perched it between his lips. The stick lighter was a Ronson art deco lighter given to the man by his mother the prior Christmas. Its base was silver and body black. Three silver bands around the left edge hinted at faux neon tubing. Garland pressed down the stick and removed it quickly. Placing the wand's lit tip to the end of his cigarette, he drew in a deep breath that brought the tobacco to life. The burning ember glowed brightly until he removed it from his mouth. "What have you gotten so far?"

"Two black males did the murders. We've got eyewitnesses saying they saw the whole thing. One was in his truck and said when the men fled the scene they stopped and threatened to kill him if he said anything."

"But he came forward anyway?"

The sheriff shook his head. "He hesitated but came in yesterday after church. Maybe God spoke to him."

"That's good."

"That's not all. Said the boys abandoned the car and ran across a field. On the other side was a waiting car to ferry them away."

"Car was stolen then?"

"Yep. A teacher at Lee High School said she left the keys in the car because a former student needed to borrow it. Now she says it was stolen."

Garland stood, took a drag from his cigarette, and walked toward the fireplace. He turned to face the sheriff. "So, the former student either set this up for the murderers to take, and blame them for stealing it, or they took it before he made it to the high school."

The sheriff nodded. "Knowing the former student, I'd go with the former."

Garland smiled. "Who is he?"

"As my mama used to say, I'll give you three guesses and the first two don't count."

The smile on the prosecutor's face grew larger. "Who is it?"

"Clyde Hysler."

"Dammit. That family is filled with fuckups."

"Yep. March of '30 Al Capone visited the boy's family and stayed at the house. That's how heavy they were into bootlegging during Prohibition."

"Hmm. And when Prohibition ended in '33, I'm sure that put a dent in the family's revenue stream."

"It certainly did."

"So, the motive was robbery?"

The sheriff shook his head. "The man had," he glanced down at his paperwork to get the exact figure, "two-thousand, seven-hundred, seventy dollars, and thirty cents on him. And it was unmolested."

"Geez, why so much money?"

"The couple cashed checks for the men at the Fruit Growers Express warehouse. It was the day before Thanksgiving, and the men needed the money for their respective celebrations."

Garland's countenance glazed over, and he repeated, "the day before Thanksgiving."

The sheriff continued with his assessment. "I'm sure these guys have fled town, but we'll track them down eventually." The man reached forth and closed the folder in front of him. "It never ceases to amaze me that people who commit to a life of crime are so damned sloppy … or either stupid."

"You solve this case, and you'll have earned a second term."

"You know, Mr. Headley, I ran on a platform of not allowing organized crime to take hold in our town, and I meant it. This family is as close as it gets."

The mention of crime families sparked the recollection of State Senator Swearingen's death in Bartow in 1931. His desire to make a trip south intensified. Even if he was forced to dissociate the two events, he would be propelled toward truth.

Knowing John Surrency's soul left his earthly form at Kings Road that day, Garland Headley made the pilgrimage to the scene of the crime. Sheriff Swift had the investigation well in hand, but the man needed a greater sense of the magnitude of the crime. Facts were being gathered by deputies and would be assembled like a puzzle. It was not that flat two-dimensional edifice he desired. For the first time in his career, he wasn't in his own head figuring motive. This case spoke more to the wider universe. Throughout his career he'd tallied many victories. Until the Surrency murders his job had become rote. Maybe he'd reached the age whereby serious consideration of his own mortality became paramount? Regardless, he knew his outlook had changed, and this man and his wife provided the catalyst for seeking a higher purpose.

The road was narrow. Its dirt surface, dampened by morning dew, caked onto the bottom of the prosecutor's shoes. He didn't mind. His rationale was to commune with the area; to gather a sense of being. The thoroughfare was bordered on one side by the field through which the two men escaped. The other side was a haphazard growing of bushes and small trees. The black mohair overcoat he wore was a gift from his parents upon graduation from the University of Florida's Law School. It was cinched at the waist to protect him from unseasonably cold temperatures.

Evidence gathered by sheriff's deputies offered exact measurements of where each body lay after the assault. He stood where he imagined the car came to rest and looked down the street at the point the assailants blocked the road. Visualizing the scene step-by-step, he watched as John emerged from his car to offer aid to his murderers. He imagined the young man brandishing his weapon and the ensuing scuffle. The driver then emerged to help his partner. He watched Mayme get out of the car, move along the shoulder and into the roadway, attempting to pull the second man from atop her husband.

Two young, strong men, thirty years their junior attacked the couple. Husband and wife fought valiantly for the protection of the other. Add in a .45 caliber handgun and the bravery shown by the couple spoke of an eternal connection.

As ethereal the connection between John and Mayme, the perpetrators on the opposite side of the equation showed themselves to be motivated by animalistic desires. Not until Sheriff Swift mentioned organized crime did it begin to make sense. Provocation appeared base and territorial. Arguments for and against capital punishment had been carried out in law school moot court settings. Every student was assigned to argue both sides during their time in school. Being made to research and develop such opinions instilled in young lawyers the duality of life. Nothing was ever cut-and-dry, until now.

Garland knew the two who perpetrated this crime deserved to be returned to the dust of the earth, buried deeply, and whose souls should never grace earth again. The only consideration offered beyond the death penalty was reserved for the get-away driver. Not until his true purpose was known would his fate be made clear.

Once the energy of the location had been fully absorbed, Garland drove from the scene to County Hospital. The drive offered more time to think. Consideration of John and Mayme's life and death helped him understand the couple had all they needed. Their love was ethereal. They had four beautiful children, and grandchildren were still being counted. Everything beyond the connection of those souls disappeared upon death. Harshly defined by societal dogma as indigent, the couple had everything they needed to embrace eternal happiness.

Once at the hospital, Garland strode the same hallway in which he'd met the couple's second daughter, Bess. He slowed his pace as he approached the room in which Mayme passed into eternity. Moving beyond the open doorway, he looked back to see if the room was occupied. It was not. Possessing the confidence of a law enforcement officer, he walked boldly into the space, moved to the far side of the bed, and looked down upon it as if he looked in Mayme's eyes.

Several moments passed as Garland played out the forty-two hours between her husband's death and her eventual demise. Comings and goings of family were imagined; made easier by having met all of Mayme's children the Saturday before.

After ten minutes Garland's daylight vigil was interrupted by a presence in the doorway. Fearing a nurse would evict him, he ignored the existence of another in the room.

The person could no longer be ignored when she called, "hello, Mr. Headley."

Garland looked up and saw a woman dressed smartly in a skirted suit, carrying an overcoat similar to his draped over her right arm. "Good morning."

The woman walked into the room and extended her hand in friendship. "My name is Margaret Slater. I'm with the FBI."

"FBI? Why are you people involved?"

The woman smiled. "Well, I'm involved because Mayme Slater is my sister-in-law."

Garland made the logical progression in his mind. 'Mayme Surrency. Daughter Mayme Surrency. Married Mayme Slater.' "Ah yes. Baby."

Margaret smiled. "Yes. Baby."

Fearing an answer in the affirmative, the attorney asked, "so, you're not here in an official capacity?"

The woman shook her head.

Once relieved of the possible presence of federal law enforcement on the case, Garland realized the woman knew him immediately. "But you know who I am?"

She looked at the man incredulously. "You're our State's Attorney. I work with the FBI. I'd be daft if I didn't know who you were."

Garland laughed. "And yet I present myself as obtuse."

The woman shook away his discomfort. "Don't worry about it."

The two stood on the far side of the bed, witnessing its emptiness. Margaret inquired, "have you found any evidence to support an arrest?"

The prosecutor smiled. "You know I can't share any details of an ongoing investigation."

Margaret retorted, "need I remind you I'm with the FBI."

"But you aren't assigned to this case." The more Garland thought about this woman's connection to the family, he was compelled to confess, "the sheriff is making great progress. I would expect arrests to happen soon." He paused. "That is, if these guys are still in town."

The woman who stood before Garland was someone he'd just met. Trust had been something he offered without question, until acquaintances proved unworthy. Skepticism emanated within his soul as he looked at Margaret. Was she the tip of the FBI tentacle that wanted into this investigation? Was she indeed related to the couple's daughter? Time would tell. Fear of losing control of a case for the first time became a consideration. Resolute, Garland stiffened to his primary objective of justice for the Surrencys.

Cold November rain stung the faces of graveside worshipers. It was the 29th of November 1936, four days after the senseless murder of John and Mayme Surrency. Specs of sleet exacerbated the cutting feeling on faces of those who came to pay respects. The couple's plots in Evergreen Memorial Gardens were immediately adjacent to sacred Jewish burial grounds.

Mourners watched as rain gathered inside sand cradles atop mounds of dirt. Earth had been voided from spaces that would embrace the couple for eternity. Density swelled to the point of pooling. When the burden became too great for the pools to hold, water cascaded down the hill like miniature rivers weaving along paths of least resistance. Finally falling like a waterfall into open graves.

The reverend's wife held an umbrella over his head to protect delicate Bible pages from inclement weather.

Miriam Enge held two-year-old Carol in her arms. The child saw the mounds of dirt as nothing more than an oversized playground. Dresses for her and Bess were sewn by the mother, and she would have nothing of their destruction. Once outgrown, they would be stored for future generations. Such were circumstances during the depression.

Ted stood in front of his father. Noble held his hands gently on his son's shoulders.

Jack Stanton, the manager of the Fruit Grower's Express stood opposite the family. Garland Headley and Sheriff Swift were in attendance. The elder Enges stood behind their son's family.

Mid-ceremony, a 1936 Plymouth stopped along the narrow path that divided rows of graves. Garland's curiosity was piqued as he felt he recognized the figure inside. It was his law school classmate, and state's attorney for Polk County, Grady Judd. The man emerged from the car and closed its door as gently and quietly as possible. The two attorneys made eye-contact and the new arrival moved slowly toward his friend.

Dual caskets were suspended above respective graves cut from the earth. Double funerals were rare, but the staff at the cemetery were able to make do with supplies on hand.

Occasional gusts blew cold raindrops from oak limbs cantilevered over the gathering. Dusted participants shivered and shook away the cold as quietly as possible. An air of reverence permeated all in attendance. Ever the skeptic, Garland Headley looked upon all faces, assessing their purpose at the funeral. Certainly, the killers would not risk showing up to admire their work. Several black faces stood out in the crowd. All men, they appeared of modest means. The prosecutor ascribed their attendance as those the Surrencys knew from the warehouse. Men for whom they cashed checks. Dollars represented life's blood for men like these during the depression.

Judd finally made his way next to his friend and colleague within the state's prosecutorial apparatus. There were no words or greetings. Silently communicated by his attendance notified Headley there was purpose to Judd's presence.

Admonitions of ever-present evil in the world propelled the service forward. Acceptance of the decedent's souls by God was requested. Throughout the service, at one time or another, every adult looked around the space wondering if the souls of their friends and relatives were present. To the person, well wishes were communicated telepathically.

At the conclusion of the service the crowd slowly dissipated. Grady and Garland moved slowly to the far corner of the area adjacent the Surrencys' graves. Beneath a majestic oak tree, the men offered casual yet familiar greetings. It had been since law school graduation at the University of Florida they'd seen one another. Working as prosecutors, each was aware of the other's ascent through the ranks, until respective promotions to lead different offices.

Most attendees remained and gathered into smaller groups. It was a Sunday, and no one was compelled by a schedule.

"What brings you on a six-hour trip to attend a funeral?" Garland asked.

Judd shook his head. "It was a little longer than that. That's why I was late." The man paused. "What brought me here?" he repeated the question. "Professional curiosity."

Headley furrowed his brow and pursed his lips. "Concerning?"

"You piqued my curiosity with that phone call the other day about Senator Swearingen. When he died, I was just an assistant state attorney. Didn't have much clout. The senator was driving home from Tampa to Bartow late one night. Story was that he lost control of his car, swerved off the road, and his front axle hit a stump. When the car stopped abruptly, he was thrown into the dashboard. The impact on his chest killed him instantly."

"Official story?"

Judd nodded. "Official story."

"So, what brings you to Jacksonville?"

Grady pointed at Mayme's coffin being lowered into the ground. "That's his sister."

Garland smiled. The two men hadn't discussed relatives on the phone. "I know."

Judd looked sharply at his friend. "And?"

His friend shook his head. "I've got nothing yet. When I heard her maiden name was Swearingen, it piqued my curiosity. Bess, Mrs. Surrency's daughter, confirmed at the hospital the two were siblings."

"And you find it odd?"

"I certainly do." Garland consciously lowered his voice so the other mourners could not hear him. "The family confirmed to me that Mayme had a drug problem that stemmed from a hysterectomy. That definitely opens the door to criminal activity."

Judd thrust his head toward the open graves. "You think he was involved?"

"Something tells me he wasn't."

"Why?"

"Well, they were an older couple who worked together."

"And?"

"And they basically spent twenty-four hours a day together. I think he wanted to be with her always in order to protect her." He shrugged his shoulders. "But who knows?"

"You don't think they've been moving drugs through the grower's express?"

He squinted and shook his head. "I don't think so. I've met with the sheriff. He and his men have had five days of intense investigation, and there has been zero indication of any criminal activity on their part. I would think something like that would have come to light. Too many men work at that warehouse."

"Maybe you're right."

"What made you think of criminal activity with Swearingen's death?"

Judd scratched the top of his head. "It's not so much the Surrencys being involved, as maybe it was who all three crossed. They kept the senator's body guarded tightly. I couldn't even get in to watch the autopsy. Color me cynical, but something tells me there was a bullet hole in that man's head."

"Have the body exhumed."

Judd shook his head, rapidly. "Not yet, I'm not comfortable. If I did that I might be the next one on a slab."

Headley did not respond. He pondered the implications of getting involved in something that might get him killed. Once he shook away thoughts of death, the epiphany struck him. "You suspect someone here, don't you?"

From his right coat pocket, Judd removed a stack of mugshots. He fanned them out to view familiar countenances he'd studied for years. As if choosing a coveted ace from a poker hand he lifted one photograph in particular. "This guy is Santo Trafficante. He's made inroads and bought off Tampa politicians." He looked directly into the eyes of his associate and spoke softly. "Do you see the man in the felt fedora standing alone?"

Surreptitiously, Garland glanced across the cemetery grounds at the man. "Uh huh."

"His name is Salvatore 'Red' Italiano. He runs the operations for Trafficante. Anything illegal. Booze during prohibition. Illegal non-taxed hooch now." He paused. "Now that liquor is legal again, they've moved heavily into gambling … bolita."

"Bolita?"

Judd nodded.

"Sheriff Swift told me some witnesses said a white boy who was big in bolita has been seen around the warehouse. I figured he was just there to satisfy the gambling demands of the workers."

"Maybe not," Judd replied as he fished for another card in his photographic deck. From it he pulled another coveted ace. "This guy is Ignacio Antinori. He's in direct competition for turf in Tampa." Grady nodded toward another funeral attendee. "See the guy slapping his gloves against his leg?"

"Yeah. He works for Antinori?"

Grady smiled impishly and shook his head. "No. That's the man himself."

Garland looked at the man again, then snatched the photograph from the hand of his friend. He analyzed the countenances thoroughly. "Son of a gun. It is him."

"If I was a betting man, and I'm not, the rumors that Trafficante and Antinori are combining forces to cover the state with illegal bolita games are true. Why else would these two be together?"

Garland smiled as his understanding grew. "Antinori and Trafficante can't be seen together."

"Exactly. This proposed association dates back to around 1931." He smiled. "Now you see why I'm so interested in the deaths of the Swearingen siblings."

Garland concluded, "the senator knew about the merging of criminal powers, tried to use his political power to stop it, and was murdered."

"It was worth the drive to confirm those two are here."

8

Deputy Starkey drove from the sheriff's office downtown to the city's outskirts. A worker at the Fruit Growers Express maintained he had vital evidence relating to the identity of the third man involved in the murder. His partner was Gary Harrison. The second man occupied the passenger's seat of the squad car.

Starkey maneuvered the car from the municipality's blacktopped roads onto the graded dirt roads that garnered less attention from local politicians. Few residents of means had the occasion to venture so far from city center. Both men had their windows rolled down and enjoyed the cool, dry, December breeze that brushed their faces and nipped at their ears. The Sun's rays held enough sway over the air to toast the men's cheeks. It was the kind of weather Floridian's embraced after long, hot, and humid summers.

The lead detective drove the car over the railroad tracks that made up the spur that linked fresh fruit to the nation. He pulled the car alongside the building. Both deputies emerged from the car and walked toward the front of the warehouse. They ascended the concrete stairs leading to the platform on which several men worked.

Men toiled daily receiving fruit from the southern part of the state, packing it in individual crates, and shipping it to destinations north. The deputies observed the situation. Many men disappeared through garage style warehouse doors, only to emerge moments later with freshly packed boxes of citrus. Reasoning presumed the arrival of a train would soon occupy all energy expended by the workers. All they knew was the name of the man who had details that may help the investigation, Christian Cordon.

The officers meandered through the men as they came and went, laden and unladen with fresh fruit. Inquiries into the identity of the man were met with tilted heads and flailing arms directing them further down the platform.

Almost to the conclusion of the building the deputies found Mr. Cordon. Introductions were made. Understandably, he continued to work as he spoke to the men.

"I don't want to go accusin' anybody, but Mr. John was always good to us. When you people confiscated our money as evidence, his family stepped forward and made sure we had money for our families' Thanksgivings. Quality people."

"I get that, but what is it you think is so pertinent to the case?" Deputy Starkey asked.

"Well ...," hesitating to cast dispersions on a friend, "you know Miss Mayme had some issues with Laudanum and Heroin?"

"We are aware of that."

"There's this white boy keeps comin' around here. He always avoided Mr. John. Didn't want anything to do with that man." The man digressed in his narrative. "Mr. John had a strong soul, and a mean right hook. No matter what problems Miss Mayme had, Mr. John stood by his wife."

"And?"

"Oh ... well, about a week, maybe two, before those boys killed Mr. John and Miss Mayme, this white boy came around here. I think he was looking to sell missy some drugs." He chuckled satisfactorily. "You should have seen that boy's face when he seen Mr. John coming at him. That cracker was scared. Needless to say, Mr. John beat the ever lovin' piss out of that boy. Youngin' deserved it."

"What did this guy look like?" Deputy Starkey lifted his notepad and held his pen firmly against it.

"Aw … he's a short little fat fu … uh, guy. He ain't no taller than five eight."

The two deputies looked at one another. Christian's description matched one they'd received from multiple witnesses in the Marietta section of town, as well as those who saw the driver of the car who sped the two murderers to safety.

One last question would increase the confidence in yet another eye-witness account. "Was the man florid of face?"

The worker's laughter border on joyous cackling. "Yes. Before and after Mr. John beat the piss out of him."

9

The trip from Jacksonville to Bartow took several hours and required overnight stay. Garland's law school roommate piqued his interest concerning the death of Mayme's brother in 1931. His prosecutorial colleague travelled all the way to Jacksonville for the couple's funeral to simply identify two men. Regardless of his friend's hesitation to pursue the five-year-old case, Garland knew truth resided in Bartow.

Senator John Swearingen graduated from Washington and Lee University's College of Law in Lexington, Virginia. He lived in Bartow since the age of five. Born in Newnan, Georgia, the boy's family moved to Bartow in a covered wagon, as there were no railroads servicing the area. The boy's father was a pioneering citrus grower in Polk County.

Swearingen was elected to the State Senate in 1924 and re-elected in 1928. Political influence was building behind the man who viewed all humanity equally.

April 18, 1931, the senator travelled home from a meeting in Tampa. Just outside Bartow he lost control of his car. It swerved onto the shoulder and leaned at a thirty-five-degree angle, but never toppled. If it had, the young senator's life might have been spared, or so declared the official story. Unfortunately, the car stayed upright and when the front axle hit a stump on the shoulder, the man was propelled into the dashboard and killed.

Mass production of automobiles had been perfected by Henry Ford in the 1920s and fueled the craze for the newest mode of transportation. It didn't take long for boastful young men who'd embraced the newest machines to gather at Daytona

Beach to race. John Swearingen became known as a regular participant in the competitions.

Grady Judd, the State's Attorney for the Tenth Judicial Circuit, accompanied the senator on many trips to the opposite coast. His interest was less about horseless carriage racing, and more about how the two men could employ influence to bring prosperity to the citizens of Polk County.

On their final trip to Daytona in February 1931, Swearingen broached the subject of capturing and prosecuting Al Capone while staying at his Lakeland summer home. The senator's hard stance on crime was mirrored by Judd. Only two short months after the Polk County prosecutor broached the subject with his staff, the senator was killed on a dark and lonely two-lane highway. Capone was convicted on tax evasion charges in October of the same year. It was supposed by the idealistic prosecutor, the hit on Swearingen was the last ordered by the gangster before incarceration.

For fear of his own life, the Polk County prosecutor hadn't mentioned the subject to anyone since that fateful day in April 1931. If there was anyone he felt could be trusted, it was his UF Law School roommate, Garland Headley. Until the funeral he would only confirm he was aware of the senator's death. Never did he speak of their friendship, or his desire to stamp out organized crime.

The prosecutor from Jacksonville approached the door and smiled. Painted on the frosted and contoured glass of the office door was his friend's name and position within the community. Fully aware the situation was the same for him in Jacksonville, his joy arose from memories of two young whippersnappers boasting about how they would conquer the world once let loose on society.

Upon entering the office Garland witnessed the sound of typewriters hammering away on carriages wrapped in paper and carbon sheets producing documents in triplicate. It was a model of efficiency. Beyond rows of desks Garland spied Judd in his office, waving through the glass window for the visitor to join him.

Headley made it across the floor and into the man's office. Their handshake was friendly and nearly developed into a hug, but decorum dictated the maintenance of composure.

"Have a seat," the prosecutor offered with a gesture of his hand.

Once seated, Garland crossed his legs, interlocked his fingers, and laid his hands in his lap. Pleasantries were dispensed expeditiously, and then came time to discuss business. "I called you the other day about Senator Swearingen."

Judd nodded.

"You came to the funeral of his sister ... killed five years later."

The local prosecutor nodded again.

"You've attempted to link both deaths to organized crime. You and I need to see this through."

The Polk County man hesitated. During their phone conversation he'd been happy to hear from his old friend and may have spoken beyond the point of security. Still feeling as though he could trust his friend, he leaned to the left, peered over the visitor's shoulder into the office where workers busied about their daily duties. "The more I think about it, the two deaths can't be related. The senator's happened five and a half years ago."

Garland shook his head. "That's all just a little too coincidental for me. It's worth the time and effort to investigate."

Judd paused and looked into the eyes of his college roommate with steely determination. The man across the desk no longer represented a friend, but a potential threat. If he shared information that triggered curiosity concerning the senator's death, no longer would worry extend to moles in his office, but to his trusted friend.

Garland watched his friend transform. "Tell me what you know, Grady." He paused. "You know more than what you said at the funeral. You're trying to scare me with mafia involvement."

The prosecutor remained stoic.

"You have the same look on your face as in law school, whenever you understood a concept that I asked about. You didn't want to share it then, because you wanted that edge on me when grades were posted."

A comment the visitor thought might elicit a smile, had no effect on the countenance across the desk. Finally, Judd admitted, "It's no longer about grades, Garland. This is life and death. The lives of my family, and anyone you hold dear."

Headley sat back in his chair. The significance of his inquiry soaked into his soul. No longer did thoughts of the case center around the procedural and prosecutorial. Linking murders had been viewed as nothing more than an exhaustion of leads. "All I know at this point is that someone hired two men to murder this couple. In my mind, that speaks to a career criminal. People of that ilk travel, and maybe had some dealings with your senator."

Grady shifted the conversation. "Do you remember when we'd go to the Ichetucknee River when we had a break from school?"

"Yeah."

"Remember the black hole?

Garland nodded. "Uh huh."

"The water was so clear we thought we could easily touch bottom. We'd dive in and swim toward the center of the hole, but never come close to breaching its outer ring." He paused. "That's what this case is like. People in higher places have control and will always prevent us from getting to the bottom of that hole. Shit disappears in that abyss."

"Do you remember my moot court appearances?"

Grady chuckled.

"I'd get pissed off if I were overruled or denied an objection." Garland smiled. "You're the one who coached me to let go of my emotion. You convinced me that sometimes the person I was prosecuting was innocent; that the system is flawed." He leaned forward in his chair and looked his friend squarely in the eye. "Your advice was the single inflection point in my career. I can look back and say, 'Grady Judd helped me become a successful prosecutor.' For that, I'm grateful. This case is just the opposite. There is something more there, and this family deserves answers."

Grady pressed his backbone firmly into his high-backed leather chair. "Aw. Tell me you haven't gotten to know the victims' family? That's cardinal sin numero uno."

The visitor's silence acted as confirmation.

Judd shook his head. "Man, you're going to get us both killed."

"We've got to do what's right, Grady."

"How can you be so sure this isn't simply a robbery gone awry?"

Without hesitation, Garland responded, "because Mr. Surrency was shot five times, and Mrs. Surrency twice."

"And?"

"The murderer only had one six-shooter. That means he emptied the cylinder and took time to reload. John had almost three thousand dollars on his person, which was left untouched. They were directed to murder the man, above all else."

The prosecutor looked around his office. A sense deep within his gut spoke to the possibility of his office being bugged. He knew only the FBI possessed that technology. Without uttering a word, the prosecutor motioned with his head for Garland to follow, and he did.

The two men walked silently into the outer office, across the floor, and through the front door. Once on the sidewalk outside Grady pointed toward the park across the street. The men cautiously looked both ways and crossed the street into the green space.

Grady spoke to the air around the men. Psychologically, he felt as though not acknowledging his friend's presence absolved him of responsibility for information spoken into the ether. Death was a likely outcome. "I'll tell you everything I know." He looked to his left, away from Garland. "John Swearingen and I used to go to Daytona. He liked racing his car on the beach. The last trip we made was in February '31. His accident happened in April. On that trip we discussed the ever-increasing presence of the illegal liquor trade in Polk County, and his district. Al Capone allegedly had a summer home in Lakeland." The prosecutor paused and looked straight ahead. "That next Monday I opened a file in my office to investigate the illegal liquor trade. The senator was killed less than two months later." For the first time Grady acknowledged his friend's presence with a glance. "I've got a mole in my office."

"If it's just a mole in your office, why the stroll in the park?"

"It's that hole in the earth under the Ichetucknee, Garland. We have no idea how deep it goes."

"We can swim it and find out."

Judd shook his head. "I'm not going swimming with you this time, my friend." He paused. The subject matter he felt compelled to broach, was something he felt the country had grown beyond. "In the Spanish American war, Senator Swearingen fought in the Immune regiment in Cuba. He fought alongside many black soldiers and grew to know them ... understand their true plight. Many things he proposed in Tallahassee rubbed people the wrong way. Those who really control things, don't want citizens working together. If we were to unite, control would be wrested from them." He paused. "You see, there are many reasons not to pursue this matter beyond conviction."

Grady stopped, and Garland mirrored his actions. The Polk County prosecutor continued. "I don't know if John Surrency was running for state office. Was he trying, in his own way, to implement the same change his brother-in-law attempted? He worked with many black men at the Fruit Grower's Express for seventeen years. Had he gotten to know them, and wanted to champion their cause? There seems to be a greater hidden hand at work here. Don't be surprised by anything you find out … if you continue to pursue this matter." Judd smiled at his friend. "One thing I am certain, time is the enemy of deception. The truth always exposes itself. We may both have to wait until we die, my friend. God willing, the truth will always be set free."

The two men walked in silence until reaching the far side of the town's square. They turned and began the journey back to the man's office.

"I still think we should try and find the truth ourselves."

"Haven't you been listening? Al Capone summered here like some rich, northern, industrialist. He owns law enforcement at every level, even while in prison." Grady paused. "There's a deputy sheriff called Bob Lazar in Panama City … in the panhandle. He's told me he personally has watched Capone's thugs unloading liquor coming from Cuba, at Rosemary Beach. He's powerless to do anything about it. Small towns like ours are best for criminal activity. Fewer people that must be bought off. Huge expanses of uninhabited land. Then they ship it all over the country. There is a power operating in the country … the world, that will never be taken down by the likes of us."

"But Prohibition was repelled in '33?"

The prosecutor drew in and exhaled. "What I've come to realize, Garland, is that politicians pass laws that benefit them. They profited from the illegal booze trade in cahoots with the mafia. When they devised another scam like the Great New Deal, they repealed Prohibition. That allowed them to point and say to their constituents, 'See. We did away with illegal booze and crippled the mafia. We're working for you.' All the while, they are getting filthy rich on the backs of taxpayers, through their mafia apparatus."

"But we are the people who can stop it."

Grady laughed. "Always the ideologue." He paused. "No one will ever be able to stop it. I've watched the FBI take over local investigations for no cause. When you realize those investigations taken over by the G-men, are those that might shed light on their true purpose for existing, it all makes sense."

The men stopped at the street corner opposite the office. "Politicians and federal types won't stop until they control everything. There will eventually be a complete takeover, if not the elimination, of local law enforcement. They'll take over the educational system and dumb down our children. Hell. They'll probably take over the office of every town's doctor and begin telling him how to do his business. It happened in Russia nineteen short years ago, and the citizens cheered it." Grady placed his hand on the shoulder of his friend. "I'll tell you to simply do your job and collect your pension."

"But what about our kids? Our grandchildren? What kind of a world would we be leaving them? A prison existence. That's what."

Garland's plea fell onto deaf ears. Grady walked across the street and disappeared into his office building without looking back. The man stood alone on the street corner staring at the building's double glass doors, wondering if his concept of justice had been a casualty of these murders.

10

December 9, 1936. Garland sat at his desk organizing several files for cases his office was responsible. The fireplace across the room contained only embers. It was the type of Florida winter morning whereby citizens awoke to freezing temperatures, only to have warmth take over once the sun's influence was felt by all. The prosecutor arrived at the office before daybreak. Questions remained whether Grady was overly paranoid. It was easy for the prosecutor to believe illegal rum was brought ashore on an isolated beach in the panhandle. Conception of the likes of Capone bringing in illicit drugs and alcohol through Tampa was difficult for the young man. After all, there were over a hundred thousand residents in the city. Certainly, if someone saw something suspicious, they would say something to law enforcement.

Emotions oscillated between doing the right thing, and feeling overwhelmed at the thought the whole damned world was corrupt. His roommate and friend instilled in him the kind of doubt that caused men to yield to imaginary obstacles. Frustrated, he arose and walked across the room, toward the fireplace. He stood for several moments poking the fire and watching embers spark and rise into the chimney. It wasn't heat he desired, but clarity. Garland scried intently, hoping for divination to intercede his dilemma.

From his desk across the room, the intercom sparked to life. "Mr. Headley. Mrs. Slater … Miss Slater from the FBI is here to see you."

Garland traversed the room, manipulated the switch on the machine and beckoned the woman inside. The man moved around his desk and took his seat as the door to his office opened. "Come in."

The woman was smartly dressed and held her overcoat folded over her arm. She extended her hand, and Garland stood halfway from his seated position, and the two exchanged a handshake. "Have a seat," he offered.

Agent Slater draped her coat over the left-hand chair and took a seat in the right. "Has the sheriff offered anything new in the murder of my sister-in-law's mother?"

Garland shook his head. "Not that I'm aware, but I have full confidence in him and his deputies."

The woman smiled wryly at the man across from her. "How was your visit to Polk County?"

The prosecutor's mind sparked with possibilities. How did she know he was in Bartow? "It went quite well. Grady and I are friends from law school."

"So, you are aware that Mayme is the sister of Senator Swearingen?"

Garland nodded.

"Aren't you going to ask me how I know all of this?"

"With all due respect, Miss Slater, I think I know exactly how you know my whereabouts. And it's quite scary."

Her smile grew and bordered on sinister. "If you only knew."

The prosecutor leaned back in his chair, interlocked the fingers of both hands, and rested them on his head. "Why don't you educate me?"

The visitor crossed her legs. The smile drifted away from her face, replaced by obvious concern. For the first time since the woman entered the room, Garland felt as though she were an ally. It pained the woman to say what came next. "We talk about the case around the water cooler every day. Obviously, there are FBI eyes and ears everywhere. I can also tell you there is an element in our office … housed on the upper floors, that have been activated. Little things like your trip to Bartow are common knowledge. The true interest by the FBI is known to maybe three people at most."

"Maybe our interests are aligned?"

"Meaning?"

"Meaning, that I think there is some element of organized crime involved."

The wry smile returned to the woman's face. "That's what I'm afraid of. That we are the tip of the spear for organized crime."

Garland was incredulous. He stood and walked across the room. Stopping at the fireplace he turned and watched Agent Slater follow him. She sat on the sofa, looked up and smiled at the prosecutor. He moved to the sofa facing her and took a seat. She allowed him to digest her comments. It was best he be allowed to formulate his own questions.

"How can that be? I mean, that's ludicrous."

"I'll admit that one is required to suspend disbelief, but there are an awful lot of coincidences necessary for my thesis to hold water." She paused. "After the Civil War there was a corporation started in DC. It was domiciled in Washington since it's not a state. As you know, our Constitution provides for states' rights. They have the right to govern themselves. This was the attempt by the British Royal family to regain control of the US. All *federal* lands are owned by this corporation, not the people of the United States who reside in states. This corporation has been slowly ... across generations ... advancing its control over the country. I'm sure you remember last year, on June 30, the Bureau of Investigation became independent, and its name changed to the Federal Bureau of Investigation? It is now controlled solely by that corporation, and the British Royal Family." The woman smiled again, but this time there was concern. "And, if you were taught this in law school, the Bureau of Investigation began in 1908 at the behest of Napoleon Bonaparte's great-nephew, Charles Bonaparte." She smiled again. "Isn't history interesting when you put all the pieces of the puzzle together? It kinda makes you realize why our government is constantly calling Russia the enemy. Russia saved us during the Civil War by parking war ships off both coasts to prevent the British and French from invading at a time when we were weakest. They also stopped Bonaparte's goals of world conquest. Because of Russia's protection of the U.S., whoever the puppet-masters are have taken a more subversive approach with us."

Incredulous, Garland sat silently digesting every word she said.

"There's a reason all these chess pieces are being moved globally. We're just coming out of a depression. People are weak and worried more about where their next meal is coming from. Edward didn't have to abdicate his throne in January. He was an integral part of the growth of Nazism in Germany. Too close to the plan. George has culpable deniability. Hitler scares the hell out of me."

Garland shook his head. "Okay, you're talking global politics, and all I'm worried about is the murder of a local couple."

"I'm here to warn you of what you're up against. When you see the FBI officially move in and take over the case, that's when you'll have confirmation there is a lot more to this story."

Garland's countenance remained curious. "I'm not sure why the FBI would be involved in local matters."

"Because it's profitable. The politicians require it to fund their payoffs. The FBI embraces it because it's an additional source of revenue. They keep records on a second set of books and use that money to fund programs they don't have to report to congress. It's that simple."

The state's attorney looked around the walls of his office, recalling Grady's fear of listening devices. "You're speaking awfully freely. How can you be sure the office isn't bugged?"

"I do have enough cache in the office … at least for now … to make sure we haven't installed listening devices … yet."

"Do you fear for your job?"

She nodded. "And my life." Pausing briefly, she continued, "but I have the angle that this was a relative. I can pepper them with questions and have a valid reason for doing so."

"What do you suggest I do?"

"Your job. Find these guys. Convict them. And when the time comes send them to the electric chair. I'll drive the bus."

The woman stood and leaned over the coffee table that separated the two sofas. Extending her hand motivated Garland to do the same. Once their farewell was complete, the woman turned and walked out of the room without a word. Garland watched as she left. Assessing what slowly became his reality. He'd witnessed a fellow state's attorney, and now an FBI agent, attempt to squelch his desire for complete truth and honesty in the discharge of his duties. Fecklessness was not a trait he'd promised the citizens of the 4th Judicial District.

11

December 12, 1936. Barely seven miles from the scene of the murder slept James Baker. Unbeknownst to him, his home on East Duval Street was surrounded by police. A misty rain illuminated by streetlights drifted and obscured the scene. Moisture was dense and forced deputies to occasionally wipe the excess from their faces as they approached the house.

Seventeen days passed since the murder. It was a deed that would live in the psyche of the most hardened man. James Baker was not that man, but he'd been successful pushing the event out of his consciousness. No longer did the man feel it necessary to hide in the Marietta section of town. An area west of city center offered a populace less likely to cooperate with authorities.

Baker worked at Merchants and Miners eight months prior to the murder. An accident on site severed his right thumb. Conscious of the deformity, he was known to keep his hand perpetually in his pocket. Shame over a missing appendage beckoned upon his psyche more so than the elimination of two lives seventeen days earlier. The man became comfortable with the deed and moved his existence back into his home, blocks from the Saint Johns River. Officers were required to travel not even a mile to affect the arrest.

A line of five officers queued at the chain-link fence surrounding the yard. The lead deputy lifted the gate fork and swung the fence open on its hinges. Silently the line of deputies entered and dispersed throughout the front and back yards to predetermined locations.

Baker lay in his bed, tightly bound inside his comforter. Acknowledgment of his deformity came during unconscious hours. Beneath the blanket his left hand gently cradled the irregular right. Protection of the wound was paramount to the man's soul. Embarrassment during daylight hours gave way to that which required safeguarding. Sparks of virtuosity flickered within Baker's soul.

Hard soles of deputies' shoes offered no traction on the cold, dew-laden grass. Areas of the yard lay baron with packed dirt and did little to minimize the slick environment in which they were forced to operate. If a chase ensued, there would be insufficient traction for deputies to run-down the younger, athletic perpetrator.

When all windows and doors to the house were covered by law enforcement, the lead detective swung the hand-held, metal battering ram into the front door. Wood splintered the juncture of the deadbolt and the frame. Once inside, the interior team made their way through the front room of the house and down the hall.

Baker sprang from his slumber and gathered himself. Slowly, consciousness of the situation grew in his mind. His first instinct was to look out of the window. Seeing two shadowy figures waiting, with guns drawn, drained the man of his verve for flight.

Slowly, the fugitive opened the door to his bedroom and made his way into the hall, hands raised. The two interior officers held their guns drawn and beaded on the man. The young criminal feared he stared at judge, jury, and executioners.

"Move toward us," the lead detective commanded.

Without a word in response, the young man moved toward the two. In his short life, crimes had become a way of life; the only manner of survival for someone incapable of envisioning a productive existence. He knew what to expect from his captors.

Once the criminal closed the gap between himself and the deputies, the second officer grabbed the man's left arm and jerked him to the ground. 1936 law enforcement was brutal and lacked finesse. Although a clear advantage had been established by the brandishing of weapons, the energy of a stilted mono-a-mono encounter drove the deputy's actions.

Once the prisoner was on his stomach, the deputy placed his knee in the back of the man and shifted the entirety of his weight to the point of his patella. The young man groaned mightily. Calls for mercy were met with the deputy's hand being placed on the back of the captive's head and pressing his skull hard into the floor. The officer balanced his weight between the two points of contact, exerting as much pressure as his body allowed.

"Let me up. You're hurting me," the young man exclaimed.

"You murdered two people, and you're asking for mercy?" the first officer asked.

The prisoner groaned. "I didn't do no killin'. Jones did."

"Who's Jones?"

The man struggled for relief. "He's the one who did the killing."

"So, you had nothing to do with it? You weren't even there?" The officer knew the answers to each question. The two deputies smiled at one another.

Fighting against the weight of the officer, the young man struggled to breathe. With a gasp he confessed, "I was there, but I didn't do any of the shootin'."

The officers looked surprisingly at each other. Once the man admitted to his crime the second deputy eased the weight placed on the man. "Who did the killing?"

The captive shook his head. "I don't know. Just some guy I ran up on that day. Said he knew where we could make a quick couple hunerd dollars."

"But you didn't take the money?"

"Naw." The prisoner hesitated. "That man was crazy … blood thirsty. Should never have took up with him."

"What's your partner's name?"

"I don't know. Think he said his name was Willie Jones."

"Wrong, and wrong."

With his face still pressed into the floor, the murderer asked, "what you mean?"

"Your accomplice's name is Alvin Tyler, and you just didn't run up on him the day of the murder. You guys were seen together weeks before the murder."

The man's body went limp, and he gave up the struggle. He issued one final plea by offering the last bit of information available that carried leverage. "I'll tell you where you can find him."

The two deputies looked at one another, again. The second deferred to the first to deliver the bad news to their captive. "We know Tyler escaped Jacksonville on the freighter Providence. We know the two of you worked together at Merchants and Marine. We radioed the captain, and the young man will be arrested as soon as the boat makes port this afternoon in Philadelphia."

Dejected, the young man shook his head to the best of his ability while still pressed to the floor. Only from the left side of his mouth could he utter, "just take me to jail."

After applying handcuffs, the deputy removed himself from the back of the young man, and then helped the man right himself. The three men walked to the front of the house, through the door, and into the front yard. The murderer stopped progress, stood motionless, and turned to the lead officer. "There's a gas station in Riverside. Can you take me there tomorrow?"

Curiously, the officer inquired, "why?"

"We stopped to get gas for the getaway car. I gave the attendant $1 but ended up pumping $1.25. I thought the dollar would cover my needs. The man was nice and said I could bring him the twenty-five cents." He paused and glanced at each of the deputies. "I just need to make that right before I go away."

12

      Officers Starkey and Harrison spent hours at the office going through stacks of evidence that had been gathered over the prior sixteen days. Every officer, and resident of Jacksonville understood the senseless nature of the murders. A husband and wife who were grandparents to four grandchildren needlessly lost their lives. More children would be born into the family and would never know their predecessors. Counsel of humans who'd experienced unique struggles could no longer be communicated to subsequent generations.

      Baker had been arrested in the early morning hours, mere blocks from the sheriff's office. Tyler was apprehended on board the Providence without incident. Both men offered testimony that did not deviate from the other. Word came from Philadelphia police that Tyler acknowledged everything Baker confessed; most importantly, that Baker had done none of the shooting. Tyler confessed he murdered both Surrencys. Seemingly forthright testimony provided the Jacksonville police contingent comfort necessary to ascribe validity to both men's assertion, they were hired by Clyde Hysler to commit the robbery. Doubts arose in the minds of collective law enforcement when they professed it was nothing more than a robbery gone awry.

      The Hysler family had been known locally for their seemingly constant run-ins with the law. Members of the clan, Tom, John, and Dan had all been arrested, and or convicted of murder in the early 1920s. Participating in the illegal manufacture and running of liquor during prohibition, their network had become so significant that Al Capone visited in March 1930, staying at the home of Clyde's father, Jim Hysler.

Sheriff's deputies knew the identity of the man who issued the contract targeting the Surrencys. He was known to drive proudly around town in his new 1936 Plymouth. Someone bridging the expanse between adolescence and manhood had contributed nothing to society yet drove around Jacksonville as a prince riding a prize steed. Disgust from law abiding residents provided the motivation to identify the man they'd witnessed driving the two assailants away from Grand Crossing on the morning of the murder.

Starkey and Harrison set out from the office in search of the young man. Unless he left town, law enforcement felt it easy to find him riding higher than a five-foot eight-inch man should. Two hundred pounds laden his small frame and rendered escape from confrontation nearly impossible.

Seemingly in an aimless manner, the deputies drove through the streets of Jacksonville. Arguments between the two centered on method. Starkey arguing, they should stay on known roads the boy travelled because he was so arrogant to think he would never be caught. Harrison insisted they focus on byways the boy never travelled. No one could be that stupid, he insisted.

Hours passed. The men's shift was nearing its conclusion when Starkey executed a left hand turn off Ellis Road, onto Ramona Boulevard. One hundred yards later, a car matching the description of Hysler's Plymouth came into view. Both men sat up straight in their seats. Resolute bodies stiffened anticipating a forthcoming confrontation. Laser-like focus on the driver of the oncoming car bore intensity toward the singular countenance in the oncoming Plymouth.

Heart pounding fear shuttered the driver of the Plymouth's soul as he knew the smartly dressed men were detectives. The young man knew his car was fast, but there was no way he could outrun the radio certainly equipped inside their vehicle.

Harrison laughed, giddily. "Did you see that florid faced boy? He turned as white as cotton. That's Hysler."

As the cars passed, the boy glanced over his left shoulder to see the car behind swinging around in the road. Without alternative, he pulled his car over and waited for the detectives to catch up to him.

Starkey accelerated and passed the parked Plymouth. He turned in front of the car and blocked its path forward. The two detectives emerged from their car and quickly made their way to the driver's side door.

"Are you Clyde Hysler?"

"Yes, sir."

"Get out of the car. You're under arrest for the conspiracy to commit murder."

"Excuse me?" he questioned, arrogantly.

"You hired Alvin Tyler and James Baker to murder John and Mayme Surrency."

"I did no such thing," the man retorted, as he emerged from his car.

Harrison grabbed the man, turned him forcefully, and pushed him against the car. He patted down the young man, searching for the murder weapon that had yet to be found.

"What are you two talking about? I have no idea who these people are."

Starkey leaned against the roof of the car so he could look Hysler in the eye. "We've got two of your friends who say you hired them to rob Mr. Surrency of two hundred dollars." The detective smiled. "We've also got a worker at the Fruit Growers Express willing to testify he saw John Surrency beating the piss out of you for selling drugs to his wife."

The detainee's face shifted from cotton-white, back to florid, and then beat red as anger captured his soul. In his low-brow and undeveloped intellect, Hysler reasoned there was no way a jury would believe two black men over him. Arrogance returned to the man's thoughts. His daddy would hire the best lawyer in town, and he would be free of this ordeal. All he needed to do was allow the situation to play out.

All three involved had been arrested. Each knew the state's proclivity for execution. Even if proven guilty of murder, the coconspirators believed the story of robbery, whereby no money was taken, would save them from the electric chair.

13

December 16, 1936, the grand jury received the cases against Alvin Tyler, James Baker, and Clyde Hysler. All three had been taken into custody with a great deal of certainty regarding culpability. Only Hysler had the financial wherewithal to make bail. Garland Headley made his way along the sidewalk in downtown Jacksonville. His stride was purposeful. In his right hand he held a briefcase with three files. Each represented a trial to occur after year's end. The man moved from his office to the county jail. The two men who perpetrated the crime had spoken openly with deputies. Law enforcement gathered more than adequate evidence to support claims by the young men they were hired by Hysler. It was the prosecutor's hope they'd be willing to speak of circumstances beyond the crime.

It wasn't his job to look beyond crimes for which he was tasked to prosecute. Unsettled thoughts stirred his consciousness realizing facts spoke to actions. Deadly actions were normally ascribed to superficial motivation. Disconnect echoed between the desire to rob the couple of two hundred dollars, as both men confessed, and the brutal manner in which they were slain. In fact, Mr. Surrency carried over twenty-seven hundred dollars. Money that was meant for the workers at the Fruit Growers Express for their holiday weekend. Money that had been pierced by bullets, and remained in the man's coat pocket as the two fled the scene.

It had been the plan for Baker to wield the gun during the holdup, and for Tyler to take the money. Roles were reversed when the former got cold feet and wanted to dismiss their arrangement. He implored his accomplice to just let him drive away. That's when Alvin grabbed the gun from the seat between the two and emerged from the car with violent intent.

Not wishing to enter the jail complex upon arrival, Garland stopped outside, placed his briefcase on the sidewalk next to him, and leaned his back against the exterior wall. He reached into his shirt pocket and retrieved an open pack of Viceroy cigarettes. He shook until one popped from the opening. Looking beyond the focus on the pack he held in his hand; he saw a tabby cat approach on the sidewalk below. An impish grin grew on the man's face. He replaced the cigarette and pack from where he'd taken both. Squatting to pet the cat with his right hand, he fumbled to unlock the briefcase with his left. Once open, he pushed aside the files and reached toward the case's bottom. Blindly feeling around, he smiled when he recognized the tactile sensation of a square box of cigarettes.

Still petting the cat with one hand, he held the box in front of his face with his left. The brand was Trommler. On its face was a Nazi drummer soldier with a swastika band around his left arm. He examined the symbolism contained on the small surface. The pack had been purchased by a friend with business interests in Berlin and was given as a gift. Garland shook his head and pulled the cellophane strip around the top. He discarded the static laden trash onto the back of the cat and watched joyously as it spun. Speed hastened and distress grew as the cat attempted to free itself of its newfound burden. The prosecutor's amusement quickly subsided as the harsh reality of the world once again took over conscious thoughts.

When he attempted to retrieve a cigarette, he felt a firm cardboard sensation against his thumb. Garland focused on the pack and pinched the piece between the nails on his thumb and forefinger. As it was retrieved the realization he'd gotten a cigarette card with his pack became clear. Adjusting it in his hand until he held it by its edges, he perceived the message portrayed. A small child handed a bouquet of flowers to a smiling Adolf Hitler. The Chancellor was surrounded by Nazi officers clad in brown shirts, wearing the same red arm band as the drumming soldier imploring the German people to war. "This guy scares the hell out of me," the prosecutor said aloud to no one, just before tossing the card to the sidewalk. He smiled as he saw it land face up. Visions of the hundreds of pedestrians a day who passed, stomping the face of evil offered great satisfaction.

The cat stopped spinning once the cellophane wrapper had been shed. It ran quickly from the threatening area. Garland snickered and finished the German cigarette. Unbeknownst to the world, cigarette sales provided a major source of funding for the war machine Hitler assembled.

Glancing toward the corner, Garland looked up the hill toward the intersection for his cat friend. Worried the feline might run into the street, he scanned the area intently. Finally, he spied his wayward friend. It had taken residence at the edge of the building. With his back toward the prosecutor, the cat peered around the building. It appeared focused on something as its tail swiped aggressively. Feline behavior piqued Garland's curiosity.

Drifting focus shifted from the happenings on the street to thoughts of the upcoming trials. Thoughts of the Surrencys were cast side when he was shaken back to reality. A vision eclipsed the corner of the building and made the turn toward him. He stood quickly, embarrassed at the casual nature he'd rested against the edifice.

Moving toward him was the most beautiful Japanese woman he'd ever seen. "Felix, you have impeccable taste," he muttered to the air around him.

She was rail thin and her posture was straight as an I-beam. As she moved closer her beauty became magnified. Her face formed a flawless inverted teardrop, rounded at the chin. Eyes were almond shaped and perfectly balanced with her every feature. Lips were plump and symmetrical. Pink lipstick offered the most subtle enhancement for a mouth viewed as perfect by the attorney.

Desperation overcame the counselor who was trained to recognize events compelling life stories forward. In her, he saw a woman of confidence. Nothing about her spoke to excess. There was a soul encased in her most perfect physique, and Garland surmised it to be worldly and knowledgeable. Intuition spoke of an association with her making sense of life. Some men never experience the epiphany inherent in beholding the perfect mate. In an age of decorum, she was worth pursuing.

Garland looked directly into her eyes as she approached. Her gaze maintained its forward trajectory. Wherever she was going, she was moving with purpose. As the young woman came level to her admirer, he walked briskly to meet her.

She noticed him in her periphery but kept her head straight, focused on her destination. The young woman shifted her eyes to watch the stranger approach.

Garland moved next to her and matched her stride-for-stride as the two moved down the sidewalk. "Ma'am?"

The girl stopped and turned to face her admirer. "Yes?"

"If you'd allow me to introduce myself?"

She shook her head. "I cannot allow that."

Garland detected only the slightest accent. "Why not?"

"It is not traditional."

What he conceived to be cute, came off as smarmy. "Jacksonville's a new city. Let's create some new traditions."

The young girl was not amused. "Good day, sir," she offered as she turned and walked away.

The intensity of her beauty did not wane with rejection. "Can I at least know your name?"

Garland's delight beamed from his countenance as he watched her stop, turn, and call back to him. "Nhi."

"I'm Garland," he called back.

She offered a muted wave from her gloved hand before turning once again and walking out of his life.

An expression of familiarity from a woman so beautiful became indelible. He once again spoke to the air around him.

"Nhi Headley. I kinda like that." At a time marked by senseless death, Garland recognized the amplification of life inherent in positive relationships.

He walked back to the exterior wall where he earlier stood, grabbed his briefcase, and entered the jail complex. At a time when the prosecutor witnessed only darkness in human souls, Nhi offered a glimpse into the intense beauty in the world.

After going through the proper checkpoints, the prosecutor found himself in a familiar interview room. He entered through a steel door with a narrow vertical window along the right side. The walls were bare and painted light green. In the center of the room was a steel table with four chairs: two on either side. The far wall consisted of bars associated with prison cells. Sounds of jailhouse doors opening and closing echoed down the hallway and alerted the prosecutor to the approach of two men he'd never met. Two men he hoped would satisfy his curiosity.

Footsteps grew closer, until both prisoners breached the corner of the wall where only bars separated the three men. They were chained at the waist and cuffed at that point. Ankle shackles limited their ability to stride. Shuffled hops were all that propelled them forward.

The prisoners stopped at the door. The guard who accompanied them, walked around the two from behind and opened the door with his skeleton key. Without a word the two young men walked to the opposite side of the table occupied by Garland. Each grabbed the back of a chair and withdrew it from beneath the table, never removing stares from the man they'd never met.

Without pleasantries, the prosecutor introduced himself. "My name is Garland Headley. I'm the one who is going to prosecute you … and Hysler."

The boys said nothing. It was twenty-seven years before Clarence Gideon took his case to the Supreme Court, guaranteeing legal representation for all. They had no inalienable right to an attorney and were at the mercy of the man in front of them, and twelve jurors they had yet to meet.

Garland pointed to the darker skinned prisoner, looked down at his open file, and asked, "you're Baker?"

"Yessa," the man answered.

He shifted to the other man. "And you're Tyler?"

The more aggressive, and self-described 'mean one' did not reply.

"I see. Well, let's get to the purpose of my visit today." He looked them both squarely in the eyes. "You've both confessed. Each of your stories matched the other's and told authorities when you," he pointed to Baker, "were in Jacksonville, and you," he pointed to Tyler, "were in Philadelphia."

"So?" The mean one grunted.

"So … I have no problem seeking the death penalty for you both. You can't afford to appeal any decision handed down, so … I have a great deal of leverage over you."

Baker looked scared. Tyler only smiled.

The prosecutor gained the understanding the latter was definitely the more seasoned criminal. Garland took note of the expressions and formed opinions of each, individually. When the men didn't respond verbally, the prosecutor continued. "Thanks to you both, I have all the facts in these files." He waved his hand over the folders. "But there is something deep within my soul telling me there is a lot more to this story." He paused to allow the two to speak, if so compelled. When they said nothing, he continued. "You were paid fifty dollars each to rob the Surrencys. That's a hundred dollars total. According to you both, Hysler said he expected the couple to have around two hundred dollars on them. So, he was going to pay you half the take? Maybe, but not probable for a young man who's known nothing but crime in his life." Garland waved his right hand as if brushing away his assertion. "Let's forget that for now. So, you go into a robbery expecting a two-hundred-dollar haul. If you had simply looked inside the dead man's coat pocket, you would have realized he had a lot more money than you expected. Over twenty-seven hundred dollars. But you didn't even look, did you?"

Baker glanced sharply at Tyler. Tyler sat expressionless, staring at the prosecutor.

"You ain't saying we set out to murder dem people, is you?" the weaker of the two pleaded.

Garland nodded confidently. "That's exactly what I'm saying."

Baker's wrist was secured near his waist. He thrust his elbow toward his accomplice and pled, "tell 'im. Tell 'im it was all about the money."

Tyler sat expressionless. Still staring down the prosecutor.

Baker faced Headley. "Look … the first thing Mr. Clyde axed us when we got in the car was if we got the money."

"They were simply keeping up appearances for your sake."

"But why?"

"Because if you knew murder was the intent, you would not have gone along with it. You're a patsy James. You were supposed to be holding the gun. Tyler was going to goad you into committing the murders, but you chickened out before the two of you got out of the car. If it was merely about two hundred dollars, Tyler here would have let you drive away." He paused. "You see, you were supposed to be in control of the car. You were supposed to be in control of the gun. That, my friend, gives your friend here an out. You go to the electric chair, and Alvin gets a little time for petty theft. It's not like he hasn't done time before." He paused to allow the weaker of the two to digest the gravity of his circumstances. "What you didn't know was that murder was the intent all along. Hysler knew it. Your buddy here knew it. And you're going to fry in the electric chair in Starke for it."

Baker pled with his friend once again. "Tell 'im. Tell 'im it ain't so."

Tyler finally broke his silence. "Der ain't nothin' this man can do for us, James."

The prosecutor applied more leverage. "Look … we know the two of you have known each other a lot longer than you told the police. This was not some simple happenstance. The two of you didn't just meet up and say, 'hey. It looks like a great day to commit a robbery.'"

"Dat's all I know'd it was." The weaker continued to plead.

Garland did not respond. He'd played his hand. Forcing leverage was not in his best interest. Tyler possessed the knowledge he needed to impair prosecution. If the Surrencys had been involved in organized crime, their sentence had been adjudicated and executed beyond the reach of his office. It was those who continued to roam the streets of Jacksonville for which he was concerned. Those intent on committing crimes would cost residents of the growing hamlet. The price would be lives and livelihood.

14

Although Prohibition ended years earlier, the manufacture and sale of illegal hooch remained profitable. Moonshine, as it became known since those distilling spirits were forced to do so by night. Replacing a lucrative revenue stream for the criminal element in town proved impossible. Petty theft, robbery, and extortion would be met by citizens adept at the use of a firearm.

John B. Hysler, the Liquor King as he was known, and uncle to the accused mastermind of the Surrency murder, was forced to increase production in order to raise money for his nephew's defense. The man never took the same car, and infrequently drove the same roads. Nothing surrounding his activities as a bootlegger was methodical.

The best criminal defense attorneys in town were retained. Once the indictment came down against the family's youngest criminal, motions for dismissal on varying grounds were filed with the court.

Leather medical bags were used to transport cash to the lawyer's office. Retainers were constantly drained by the furious nature of young Hysler's defense.

Alvin Tyler and James Baker's fates were left to the skills of a public defender.

The post-holiday season of 1936 saw no decline in demand for illegal, cheap hooch. It was a cool January morning in 1937, and the Liquor King was driving lonely two-lane roads west of Jacksonville. The man drove his car, laden with illegal liquor, west along Pritchard. The car had been modified by the best mechanic in Daytona. He was the go-to mechanic for men who raced cars along the beach; able to drain every ounce of horsepower from stock engines. For people inquiring of his skills, the man's usual response was, "The only thing that will prevent you from winning any race is your own fear."

Anxiety over possible arrest was mitigated by the fact most deputies were allowed to supplement incomes through kickbacks. Sheriff Swift knew prostitution and the illegal alcohol trade would endure. His goal was to make sure organized crime stayed out of Jacksonville. In his mind, outsiders allowed to prosper were there to extract from the town's residents. Friends and neighbors could innocently provide for each other's needs. Compassion was offered neighbors who allowed alcohol to grip their souls. Carpet bagging mafia tactics drove ever increasing extortion without empathy.

It was 5:00 AM. Making deliveries before sunrise cloaked the activity of bootleggers. Few deputies wanted to pull that shift.

All of the windows in Hysler's car were rolled up tightly. The cold January morning bit at the man's soul. The collar on his coat was flipped up and wrapped tightly around his neck.

The man's car left the blacktopped section of road. He drove the desolate dirt portion with ever-increasing comfort. Although his eventual destination was Lake City, he drove a road that skirted north toward Nassau County to offer a potential means of escape. His cargo was destined for the small port village of Panama City. A portion of the load would stay in the area to service the vices of residents. The balance would be shipped west to New Orleans.

Hysler negotiated the bend northward. Darkness ahead offered continued comfort he was alone. Traveling in solitude another mile, the man negotiated a slight westward bend. Once clear of the pine trees lining the road, his heart skipped as headlights appeared in the distance. "Maybe it's a farmer delivering to the market in town," he thought. He slowed the vehicle's pace to assess the identity of the party occupying his route.

Inside the passing car were the countenances of two deputies he met with weekly to grease their palms. Unrecognizable was the third man who occupied the back seat behind the driver. The oncoming car slowed its pace as well. All three made the identity of the lone driver. All four men stared intently, assessing the situation and how to proceed.

The criminal knew the two men carried the potential for arrest. Charges would be dropped with a warning; all to support the narrative that crime was being fought. It was the third that worried him to the point of pressing the accelerator to the floor. Rear tires spun until they gripped the compact, hard base beneath surface sand and propelled the vehicle far into the distance. Looking backward over his shoulder he saw the car turning to give chase.

Constantly assessing the gap between the two cars, John B. drove fast in the straightaways, slowing only to make turns. A seventy-degree turn lay ahead that shifted the path southwest. He slowed to allow for a more in-depth assessment of the men chasing him. He shook his head in disgust as he saw the car continuing to give chase. He hoped they wouldn't be able to properly negotiate the turn. They did.

An exaggerated S curve lay ahead. Maybe he could lose them there? Heading south there was a smaller set of curves before the road merged onto Chaffee Road. Accelerating toward one more small elbow turn, Hysler made the corner like a pro. He propelled the car toward the curve, slowing only to check the progress of his pursuers. Thirty seconds later, curiosity burgeoned within as headlights never materialized behind him. Boldly, the criminal stopped his vehicle, got out, and walked back along the road searching for deputies he knew well.

After a hundred yards of progress the man saw headlights illuminating the trees along the side of the road. "They're in the ditch," he thought, and grinned satisfactorily.

Shifting his position to the near side of the path, Hysler continued to the road's bend. There he stopped and witnessed the car stuck along the side of the road. He confirmed the two were his deputies. The third man was unrecognizable.

The man squatted in place, debating how to handle the situation. The two had the power to make his life hell, yet he had a delivery to make. Hysler picked up several rocks from the road's surface and tossed them one-by-one, never aiming at anything. He thought of his nephew and the need for additional money.

"The money can wait one more day. These guys can put me away if they become angry enough with me."

Hysler jogged back to his car and drove away. Traversing Chaffee Road beyond Florida Highway 228 until it merged into Samaritan Way, the criminal had a friend who owned a farm. He left his alcohol laden car in a barn, behind several bales of hay. The farmer loaned him a clean car, which he drove back to the scene of the accident that stranded the three men.

Hysler pulled the clean car beyond the stranded vehicle as the three watched his progress without a word. He executed a three-point turn and brought his automobile to rest on the shoulder in front of the disabled car.

Without mention of the chase by any of the men, Hysler offered, "I've got a chain in the trunk. I can pull you out."

"We'd appreciate that," the lead deputy responded.

No other words were spoken between the men as the criminal removed the chain from his trunk. He crawled beneath both cars, attaching the chain securely to the undercarriage of each.

After freeing the car from its predicament, Hysler repeated the steps necessary to free the two cars from their tether. The man replaced the chain in his trunk and walked toward the driver's door.

The lead deputy called to the criminal. "Thank you, John B."

Law enforcement appreciation was met with a wave as the bootlegger got into his car and drove away.

The third man, a federal liquor agent, questioned, "why didn't you arrest him?"

The lead deputy offered, "in case you didn't notice, there was no alcohol in that car."

Disgustingly, the third man grunted, turned, and walked toward the car. Over his shoulder he shouted back at the two deputies, "guys like that should be shot."

15

Margaret Slater walked the long hallway of the FBI field office in Jacksonville. Her heels, influenced by the gate of her walk, made a rhythmic cadence announcing her presence to all who listened. Typewriter keys pounding along carriages echoed as she passed opened doors of offices. Each individual space represented an area of north Florida, Alabama, and Georgia the office serviced. Reports were brought in from the field and typed to maintain permanent records.

Agent Slater had been summoned to the lead agent's office. Since the arrest of the chief conspirator in the murder of her sister-in-law's mother, inquiries had been made into the agency's interest. The newest generation of a well-known local crime family ordered the robbery of a man who ended up dead. As facts emerged, the mosaic of evidence composed a portrait that spoke to more than robbery gone wrong.

The two young men who'd committed the murder had a history of petty crimes. Graft and theft seemed to be the extent of their juvenile criminal careers. It would have been easy for the two twenty-somethings to overpower a man of sixty-two. Strong armed robbery would have fit their modus operandi, and not triggered a single question. Deadly force was too quickly relied upon in the situation. Margaret's critical mind simply couldn't dismiss all that was contrary to the narrative espoused by law enforcement.

Agent Slater opened the door to the outer office of the agent in charge of the Jacksonville office. His secretary had her back to the door. She faced her typewriter on the desk return and banged away upon its keys. Noise prevented her from recognizing someone entered the room.

Dutifully, Margaret stood and waited to be recognized. Several moments expired and she walked around the corner of the desk, into the secretary's vision.

"Oh, Agent Slater," the woman recognized the investigator after being jostled into the reality surrounding her. "Mr. Thompson is ready to see you. Go on in."

"Thank you," she replied, as she made her way to the office door. Slater tapped lightly with the knuckle of her right index finger, on the upper opaque, glass section of the door. It was emblazoned on three lines and announced the space's occupant, *Harold Thompson, Agent in Charge, FBI – Jacksonville.*

"Come in," bellowed a voice from inside.

Margaret opened the door, walked across the floor, and sat in the right-hand chair of two positioned in front of the man's oversized mahogany desk.

Harold stared through his window and onto Duval Street. With his back to Agent Slater, he spoke. "I hear you're asking a lot of questions about the Surrency murder?"

"Yes, sir."

"That is a matter not being investigated by this office."

"Yes, sir. I understand that."

"Would you mind telling me why this murder seems so interesting to you?"

"Nothing about it adds up to robbery. The guy who contracted the murderers is the youngest in a long line of bootleggers … and murderers, I might add. The initial story of the assailants is falling apart. At first, they told deputies they only met the day before the murder. Witnesses in Marietta state the boys have known each other … and committed crimes together for years. Bolita was the most serious crime they'd committed to date. All of a sudden they graduate to murder?"

Margaret shook her head emphatically, even though Thompson couldn't see her. "I'm not buying it."

"Miss Slater, is there anything about this case you do believe?"

"Yes. I believe Baker when he says he had no intentions of murdering Mr. and Mrs. Surrency. He was merely to hold the gun on Mr. Surrency while the more physical Tyler attacked Surrency to take the money."

Agent Thompson drew in and exhaled a deep breath. "So, you think Tyler could easily have graduated to murder, but not Baker?"

She nodded. "I guess that's exactly what I'm saying. He seems to possess a murderer's bent. An anger for his own existence that manifests in destruction of others."

Something caught the eye of the agent in charge on the street below. With his right index finger, he pulled down a couple slats of Venetian blinds and stared without comment.

"Is that all?"

"No."

Margaret sat silently, waiting for her boss to rejoin the conversation.

Thompson released the pressure from the blinds, and they snapped back into place. "Stop inquiring of local law enforcement about the Surrency murders. It's a local matter, and I'm certain they are capable of prosecuting these young men … all three."

"But sir, I have a vested interest in the case."

"How?"

"My sister-in-law is Mayme's youngest daughter."

The man snapped around. A worried look crossed his countenance only briefly. Quickly, he was able to disguise concern with an empathetic gaze. "Why didn't you say anything? No one in the office knew you were related to the victims." It was a lie. The man walked around the corner of his desk and stood over Margaret. The man held out his hands compassionately and lifted her from her seat. What was demonstrably kind-hearted was intended to hasten her exit. Warnings about her continued interest in the case had been issued. As he walked her toward the door to his outer office, he contradicted the intent of their meeting. "You go ahead and keep us all up to date with everything you find out about this case."

Somewhat dubious, Margaret agreed. "I will, sir."

Thompson stood in his open doorway as he and his secretary watched Agent Slater exit the office. The echo of the door closing hadn't dissipated before the G-man barked at his secretary, "get J. Edgar on the phone."

16

Clyde Hysler's first trial was for the murder of John Surrency. It began the third week of January and continued for three weeks. A plea of not guilty had been entered in the middle of December when indictments were handed down. The third-generation criminal's contention was, he had no idea who the two men were who committed the murder. His view of the black community was that of a race to be used for dirty work which he didn't wish to associate. Confidence oozed from pores of the pasty white thug.

Motion after motion had been serially filed by the best defense attorney money could buy. Ill-gotten gains provided a financial war chest deep and wide. Throwing legal excrement against the wall hoping something would stick was only half the strategy. Garland's stamina would be tested. Defense attorneys hoped the man would tire and make a mistake. The state's attorney was severely underestimated by the opposition.

It was the prosecutor's hope to one day have a large family like the Surrencys. Miriam and Noble Enge had been gracious and invited him to their home to participate in a salvaged Thanksgiving. The man worked too hard for adequate courtship. Relationships never advanced beyond meeting women who struck his fancy. Baby Surrency had been one of those women. She was married. The search for a life mate continued, as did his determination to prosecute the men who destroyed the concept of family, which he coveted.

Undeterred by a constant barrage of court filings, objections to jury pools, and motions to dismiss on a myriad of grounds, Garland Headley moved forward with prosecution. His case was built brick-by-brick, upon a sound foundation of eyewitness accounts. Events that spoke to the defendant's involvement were brought forth. As a law student, Garland and his classmates complained of the abundance of assignments given by professors as busy work. It was times like these he appreciated higher standards. Intense focus and continued tenacity were what it took to be a good lawyer. Singular focus upon justice for the Surrencys pushed aside all other aspirations.

Regardless of the fact both men who committed the crime testified Hysler offered to pay them fifty dollars each, Garland would not leave conviction to chance. Their stories remained without equivocation from the moment of arrest through trial.

Sheriff's deputies worked tirelessly canvasing the town gathering evidence, and eyewitness accounts. It was a town possessing a great deal of potential. Sheriff Swift and his deputies understood they'd been placed at this moment in history to secure Duval County's future.

James Baker testified Hysler told them to rent a car to commit the murder. When it was learned that black folks couldn't rent a car, the white man arranged to borrow the car of a teacher at Robert E. Lee High School. A woman with whom he'd had a relationship was willing to offer her vehicle, for what purpose she had no idea. Baker never felt comfortable carrying out the crime and attempted to back out several times. Each instance was met with the declaration by Hysler that if the crime was not committed, he would blow the man's brains out.

Extensive maps of the area were brought in by experts and entered into evidence. The dirt road in Grand Crossing was highlighted as was the field across which the two assailants fled to meet Hysler on the other side. Both men testified to the route taken by Hysler to escape. The two were dropped off in Cracker Swamp, and told never to speak of the event, "even to a grasshopper."

Both men held up under cross examination from two attorneys for the defense. Facts were recounted without contradiction. Baker even went so far as to confess, "I never had any idea I'd ever be a free man and if I died that would be one thing that didn't worry me."

Baker admitted once that someone involved in the trial had tried to influence his testimony. He pointed out Colonel Anderson, co-defense counsel. "When we were out at the state pen in Raiford, he got up and shook his finger in my face and told me I was a damn liar if I say somebody didn't promise me something for making this statement, and said I was going to burn for it." A satisfied grin widened across Headley's face. Without realizing it, the defense team admitted their fear of law enforcement attempting to take down a crime family. In an ever so slight manner, he was able to indirectly introduce a family whose history involved prolific wrongdoings.

Once the men were dropped off in the swamp, Baker testified Hysler told them he needed to get back to town and tell Laura Newsome, the former Lee High School teacher, to report her car was stolen.

Both men had been seemingly honest throughout the process. Once again, Garland felt Tyler held his cards close to the vest. Baker reported that ten days after the murders, Hysler asked him to meet in the swamp because he needed to show him something. At a time when the three criminals felt the heat of law enforcement closing in on them, the white man resigned himself to eliminate one man who could testify to his involvement. Baker said he didn't keep the meeting because he'd seen a shotgun in Hysler's car. When asked if he feared for his life in the same manner as his accomplice, Tyler simply shook his head. Unknown leverage emboldened confidence in the meaner of the two.

Three ladies testified to witnessing the shooting. Mrs. Laura Green, Miss Barbara Atkinson, and Mrs. T.J. Baxter all said they saw Tyler shoot the Surrencys. The assailants then drove the car owned by Lee High school teacher Newsome to the end of the road. At which time they emerged, jumped the fence, and ran across a field to an awaiting car on St. Clair Street.

A.B. Cox, a driver-salesman for the local Coca-Cola bottling company testified to seeing the murder of the Surrencys and confirmed that Tyler was the one who committed the murders. When the men drove by his delivery truck, they stopped and told him if he said anything of the murders, they'd kill him.

Pressed by defense attorneys, Mrs. Wainwright, admitted she had a grudge against Clyde Hysler. The woman had seen the three men together at a gas station at 10:30 on the morning of the murders. Her son was serving time in Raiford for a crime committed by the defendant. The boy had stolen a car in St. Augustine, for which her son was accused. Hysler made many empty promises to rectify her son's situation. He promised bail, that never materialized. He promised to appeal the son's conviction, which never materialized. Clyde Hysler displayed a history of having others commit crimes on his behalf, or at least take the fall. Defense attorneys gloated at proving the woman's hatred for their client. In reality they brought awareness to the kind of human who ordered murders to remain void of accountability.

Theresa Hicks, an attractive Lee High School student testified she saw Baker and Tyler driving away from campus in Mrs. Newsome's automobile.

Jacksonville Police Officer, Dick Gore testified he'd seen the murder weapon several times in Hysler's possession. The weapon's existence began at Bazzar's Main Street Bar. The proprietor asked if the officer knew of someone who he could trade the .45 caliber for a smaller handgun.

Joe Byrd, a roofer by trade had used the gun for securing a ten-dollar loan from the saloon owner. The man testified he'd made several marks on the left-hand side of the handle, which were identified in court. Also present were recognizable marks on the trigger guard, from where the gun hung on a nail beneath Bazzar's bar. When he couldn't pay back the loan, he allowed Bazzar to keep it in full payment of the debt.

Ownership of the gun was then transferred to Jim Hysler, the defendant's father.

Witness after witness after witness corroborated testimony of others who'd seen the murders. From every conceivable angle, workers had seen what Baker and Tyler did to the Surrencys. Garland Headley successfully traced the lineage of the murder weapon and placed it in Clyde Hysler's hands. The prosecutor aligned all facts against the man who directed the senseless murders.

Robert B. Walsh, a witness for the defense, was arrested for perjury thirty minutes after testimony. It was the first in a murder trial in the state of Florida. The man testified Hysler had not been at the gas station with the two assailants the morning of the murder, when in fact he had. Regardless of the challenges faced by the state's attorney, he maintained focus and weathered all objections and shenanigans of the defense team.

The trial began on January 21, 1937. It was February 12th and the jury returned with their verdict. The twelve men took ten hours and fifty-two minutes to deliberate several weeks' worth of evidence and testimony. The verdict in the first-degree murder of John Surrency was guilty, but with a recommendation to be placed "to the mercy of the court." There was no way the judge would sentence Hysler to death in the electric chair, against the jury's recommendation. Three and a half weeks of intense work. No stone was left unturned, yet Garland failed to achieve an eye for an eye. Sleepless nights would be spent between the first and second trials. There was no way Headley would allow this man to go unpunished for his crimes.

Garland sat at the defense table stunned. The only question for which he had no answer was, "why?" Why was a man so obviously callous and guilty not given the death penalty?

Why was the $2,700 not taken in what those involved called a robbery? Why did Baker fear for his life at the hands of Hysler and Tyler didn't? Why did Tyler insist on carrying through with the crime when Baker got cold feet? Tyler appeared to be more connected to the overall apparatus than did his accomplice. There was an invisible hand at play. What the prosecutor had yet to understand was those within his own sphere of influence created the current against which he struggled.

17

March 15, 1937. The trial for the murder of Mayme Surrency began in the Duval County Courthouse. Hysler's attorneys argued they would not have sufficient time to prepare the case. A motion for continuance was denied by Judge Shields, saying the court had just concluded a trial for the exact same case. Defense should be fully prepared.

Desire for the death penalty in the case was great. Headley felt a failure in not securing such a sentence in the prior trial. Every difference in the two deaths at the hands of the same men would be exploited. All projectiles fired from the murder weapon cleared the body of John Surrency. Nothing linked the murder weapon physically to the male victim. Fate intervened in that a bullet lodged in the spine of Mrs. Surrency. D.J. Parsons, a ballistics expert from the F.B.I.'s Washington D.C. office testified the bullet taken from Mayme's spine was fired from the gun held out as the murder weapon in both trials.

Fifteen additional witnesses were called by the prosecutor. Every angle of testimony would be utilized in making this trial a success. Success was only defined by death.

Initially, the trial was slated to include all three men involved in the murder of Mrs. Surrency. Lawyers for Alvin Tyler and James Baker successfully argued for severance, allowing the two criminals to be tried separately.

In the short time between trials for murder of husband and wife, James Hysler, the defendant's father, had been convicted and sentenced to a year and a day in the Atlanta Federal Penitentiary on alcohol tax charges. Defendant had been declared insolvent, so the cost of bringing the patriarch to testify would be borne by Duval County. The cases of John and Mayme Surrency contained many legal firsts; including the issuance of a writ of habeas corpus ad testificandum from Florida's Attorney General. It was addressed to the prison warden of another state, bringing the elder Hysler across state lines to testify.

Defense attorneys for the ringleader of the conspiracy filed a motion in favor of the writ on Tuesday March 9, 1937. It was necessary to have Hysler's father testify, but have the county pay for all expenses. On Wednesday March 10, 1937, the defendant's attorneys filed a motion questioning the court's authority to issue such a writ. Absurd legal fees were spent making every possible challenge to authority, by a young man deemed destitute.

Even Charles Ponzi made an appearance in court via precedent setting rulings. The inventor of the scheme, whereby old investors were paid a return from the money secured by new investors, had profligate dealings during the north Florida land boom. There had been a writ issued in his case that allowed him to cross state lines. The crook was brought into court from the custody of a federal prison, in order to testify in his case. That summons withstood the scrutiny of the United States Supreme Court and was applied to the Hysler patriarch's appearance in court.

Objections to jury pools, change of venue requests, and a myriad of challenges to witnesses did nothing more than delay the inevitable. Three venires, each of at least one hundred potential jurors, were drawn in order to satisfy the challenge-happy defense. An objection was levied concerning the fact some slips may have been left in the jury box before subsequent draws. Jury selection carried the trial into its second week. The defendant, declared bankrupt, had no problem spending legal fees marshaling feeble attempts to deny justice.

The addition of Leonidas Wade to the defense team happened once the testimony of witnesses began. Mr. Wade was a well-known defense attorney from Green Cove Springs who'd acted as counsel for Tom Hysler, the defendant's uncle. The attorney successfully argued an acquittal for the man in a 1905 murder case.

No detail was cast aside as desire for the death penalty echoed within Headley's soul. He even brought in an additional witness to testify she'd seen the .45 caliber murder weapon in Clyde Hysler's possession. Mrs. C.W. Bowling of Tallahassee had been on a date with the defendant and swore to the fact the gun involved in the commission of the Surrencys' murders was in his car the night they were together. Every reason, no matter how seemingly insignificant, for twelve jurors to recommend death was brought forward in trial.

Upon conclusion of testimony for both prosecution and defense, attorneys for the defendant claimed to have an additional witness with blockbuster information. That witness never materialized. Tactics. Testimony from the defendant's father, who attended all three weeks of the trial at the county's expense, was never heard.

Garland's closing argument to the jury included his promise to bring Alvin Tyler and James Baker up on the same charges and request the death penalty. "No promises were made to either man for leniency. Nothing compelled these men in their testimony other than their conscience and becoming right with God before their demise."

April 6, 1937: "And we recommend him to the mercy of the court," was a phrase absent the jury's verdict of guilty. Chills shuttered the soul of Garland Headley and manifested in goose-skin by the lack of leniency declared by Hysler's peers. Automatic fixation of the death penalty was assured.

18

Jacksonville breathed a collective sigh of relief. The most heinous murderers in the history of the hamlet had been tried and convicted. Competing newspapers covered the trial in great detail. Death of an innocent couple garnered boundless attention and possessed the energy to make or break all manner of entity. Survival of the media, the sheriff, prosecutor, and even the town itself depended on making sure citizens felt informed and safe. Truth has a spirit unto itself. Its frequency is pure and without border; ebbing and flowing through those who seek it and speak it. Disrupted honesty possesses a visceral impact which cannot be forgiven.

Garland Headley successfully prosecuted the ringleader of the crime that ended in the death of husband and wife. Legal briefs were detailed, and witness lists were long. Sheriff Swift and his team of deputies left no stone unturned in their investigation. Separate trials for John and Mayme offered isolated baskets into which the prosecutor placed his fortune. Approaches to jury selection were different. Opening statements and summations varied based on the message he wanted communicated and heard. The goal was singular. Headley would do anything in his power to ensure the ringleader, the catalyst for the murders, would be put to death in the state's electric chair. The stakes were too high to risk on a singular roll of judicial dice.

As the prosecutor feared, the jury in the trial for the murder of John came back guilty, with a recommendation for mercy. The judge honored the guidelines set by the jury and set the sentence at life in prison.

Like a chess master, Garland Headley examined every sentence contained in the court reporter's record. Background associated with every jury member was examined in greater detail when performing Mayme's voir dire. Had he missed something? Were any of the jury members associated with the mafia? The Hysler family had money. Were members of the jury paid for leniency? Recurring questions drove the man to exhaustion between trials. Work had become central. Rarely did he go home for even a change of clothes and a shower. Florida winters provided an environment conducive to a few days without hygiene. Whore's baths were taken in the lavatory down the hall. Only upon the insistence of Miss Goldman did Garland go home for a few hours to shower and rest in a bed that wasn't a sofa.

Passion for justice was pure within the man. Unknown circumstances presented that which was outside his control. For all of his work, machinations behind the scenes usurped control over the justice in which he believed.

Without the prosecution's knowledge, Alvin Tyler requested a meeting with the head of the Jacksonville FBI office. The murderer's appeal was granted without hesitation.

Four burley, suit clad agents gathered the young man from the jail and transported him to the FBI building. The prisoner's black and white striped jumpsuit had been exchanged for a brown flannel suit and fedora pulled down over his brow to hide facial features. The wiry young man was sandwiched between two massive agents in the back seat of the government automobile for the trip between buildings.

Their route inside took them through a rear stairwell that deposited the five men into the corridor outside the director's office.

Margaret Slater emerged from the office as the leader of the five jerked the heavy wooden stairwell door open. She had been delivering a summation of reports from the prior week. Startled, the woman moved aside as the agents encircled the prisoner. Seeing the young black male hidden between coworkers piqued the woman's curiosity enough to exacerbate her stare. There was only a partial profile beneath the fedora, but enough to recognize for the woman whose relative had been murdered by the young man. She kept a copy of his mugshot in her desk and stared at it daily. She memorized the shape of his jawline, and every line on his face.

The woman rushed back to her office before the vision faded. She dropped paperwork on her desk. It fanned out and slid onto the floor. She didn't care. Her purpose was singular. Quickly she jerked open the long, narrow, center drawer of her desk. Staring up at her was the face she encountered in the hallway. She lifted the visage from its lower right-hand corner. Holding the picture between her thumb and forefinger, Margaret furrowed her brow. Why was the young man who'd been arrested by local authorities, in a case in which her office was not involved, being taken to the director's office?

The mass of men that girdled the county's prisoner moved quickly past Director Johnson's assistant and into his office. The FBI director stared through his office window onto the green space below. He stood stoically, not disturbed by the commotion that populated his office. The criminal was not unknown to the man.

A gap in the circle materialized almost organically at the point of one chair in front of the director's desk. The prisoner sat.

"You gentlemen can leave us alone," the director commanded, without removing his gaze from the street below.

The four men exited the room and waited in the outer office for additional marching orders.

Still not facing his guest, the director asked, "You called this meeting. What is it you want from me?"

"Dey gave Hysla' def. I don't want no def."

The director turned slowly. Asserting superiority he bellowed, "you murdered a man and his wife. Baker admitted it.

You admitted it. You did all of the shooting. No one else held the gun. You did."

The young man shifted the hat, so its front rim rested high on his forehead. He sat back into the chair, resigned to stay as long as it would take to convince the man. Assurances no death penalty awaited him were all that prevented embarrassing disclosures from coming forth.

The director moved to his chair and sat down. Resting both elbows on its arms, he steepled his fingers just below his chin. "Hurry up and tell me what you want. We've got to get you back to the jail before those we don't control find you missing."

"I don't want to go to jail."

The G-Man laughed. "There's no way I can make that happen."

"I ain't never been arrested for all the other crimes you had me commit. Why now?"

The director sat sharply forward. He rested his right elbow on the desk in front of him and thrust his finger over-and-over. "Don't you ever … and I mean ever, speak of our association again. You've been well compensated. Transactions happen, and they're forgotten."

"Ain't nobody forgettin' dis one."

The old man sat back and relaxed into explaining the facts of life in Jacksonville. "We have an overzealous sheriff in town. Constitutionally, he's the highest officer in the county. He's prevented us from infiltrating the power structure in town." The man interlocked his fingers and held them on the back of his head, with his elbows spread out. "Son, you're just going to have to deal with it."

The criminal shook his head quickly, in short bursts. "Naw. Naw. That ain't happenin'."

Smugly, the man continued. "You've confessed to the murder. It's been reported in all of the papers. Every citizen in Jacksonville knows you murdered an innocent couple. No matter what they were into, that's how they perceive the story." He released his right hand and began gesturing. "Even if I could wave my magic wand, and open the doors to that jail, and set you Scot free, these people would hunt you down and hang you. It would probably be the most justified hanging in the history of these forty-eight United States."

"You took my meetin'. You know all the information I have about this office and how it operates, I can make a lot of trouble for you and Mr. Hoover."

"You're not going to do that, because then your life wouldn't be worth spit."

"Whatch ya gonna do for me?" He held his palms level, and skyward. He bounced his left hand. "I got all this information in dis hand." He bounced his right. "Whatch you gonna put in dis one?"

The men stared at one another before the director responded. "The best I can do for you is guarantee you won't be executed. I can get you into a federal prison that I control." The G-Man smiled. "Three hots and a cot for the rest of your life."

Questions remained in the criminal mind. "You bound by Duval County?"

The man shook his head. "No. I'm federal. I can work all over the US."

The young man hesitated. "The worst thing I did was murder that senator in Bartow for you."

Yelling, the FBI man snapped back, "I told you not to mention our association ever."

Disregarding the threat, the young man expanded on the murder. "I murdered that man, and you were true to your word that you could make it look like an accident."

"So, what's the problem?"

"Inmates tell me that senator was the brother of Mrs. Surrency. I know a lot about you, but dat ain't nothin' but pieces to a puzzle. Dat's how you like it. Nobody sees da full pictcha. I'm certain if this information got out, people who's a lot smarta than me … and even you, could find out what was really goin' on."

Reaching into his drawer, removing a pistol, and shooting the threat that sat before him was briefly considered by the director. Intellect took over when he realized the young man was too high profile. Elimination must be disguised in the form of a jail riot, or some other unforeseen accident. "Like I said earlier; three hots and a cot is the best I can do."

19

Alvin Tyler's energy shifted when the verdict came down. Its culmination would result in the death of the man who hired him. Having been the only person to pull the trigger that day before Thanksgiving, he was certain the same fate awaited him. Doubts filled his psyche. Was he valuable enough the FBI would aid his escape from justice? He knew the organization wouldn't blink an eye in ordering the execution of any crime that furthered their agenda. There were many associates who would perpetrate crime for the generous pay the G-Men offered. He was certain there were many white men who would have done the same during the time of the depression. His only saving grace was the leverage provided by knowledge relating to crimes past.

The black section of the Jacksonville jail was set up like army barracks. Bunk beds lined each wall and ran the length of the room. A center aisle bifurcated the room. At one end the wall consisted of cell bars and a door that led into the greater jail complex. At the other were bathrooms and showers. A set of three barred windows were positioned equally along each wall. One set looked onto the exercise yard and one onto the street that led to freedom. Men stared out, imagining themselves walking away from the building and the trouble they'd created for themselves.

News from the prior day that Hysler had been given death for the murder of Mayme Surrency echoed constantly in the man's soul. He knew Garland Headley had been smart to try the two cases separately to increase the odds of getting death for at least one murder. Tyler had been the only one directly involved in ending the couple's lives. Reflections of his life as a criminal offered the realization, he'd been destined by circumstances. Meanness had been instilled in him as a child of poverty. It hadn't taken long into his development as an adolescent to become aware he could control those around him through fear. Its intensity brought forth greater autonomy. He witnessed destitute members of his community struggle to keep food on their tables. Inner dialogues spoke to the fact Tyler valued himself more than most. Anger and hatred passed down through generations diverted the man's energy. He possessed the requisite intellect, if coupled with hard work, that would have set his life on a fruitful path. Instead, each subsequent generation buckled under dogma. Tapping inner malice was easy and encountered fewer obstacles.

The fact that Tyler's life of crime culminated in murder surprised no one, least of all the FBI that used him as a shadowy tool.

Walls have ears, and words were never spoken advancing tactics until the last possible moment. Time for second thoughts were not allowed. Nor was the potential for communicating with others possessing the potential of becoming state's witnesses. Operations were swift and decisive.

Tyler sat atop his upper bunk. Knees were bent and lower legs dangled over the wooden framed bed. He stared through the window onto the exercise yard. His eyes traced the outline of the wall that confined the space. Walls at Raiford were three times as high as the county jail and were manned by armed guards. A lifetime of incarceration appealed to the man more than the eventuality of having two thousand volts of electricity burn his organs to the point of failure. He'd taken two lives. It was an act he never considered until approached by the FBI. The deed paid ten times better than any job he'd fulfilled for the agency. For a man who'd never reached a spiritual level within himself, money seemed to fill the void. Avarice rendered him incapable of viewing human life as valuable. His only concept to life was physical, and he wished his earthly manifestation to exist as long as possible. If the FBI came through and helped him obtain freedom, he would show gratitude by continuing his role as a tool for as long as they required.

Men milled about the space around Tyler. It was overcrowded and some men were made to sleep on mattresses scattered about the floor. Complete disregard for optimal sanitation led to a rules-based society amongst their ranks. Tyler's mean streak coupled with the fact he was the only one who'd committed murder cast him in the role of enforcer. Men took turns sweeping and mopping. Latrine duty was reserved for newcomers.

Tyler's time in the facility approached five months, which was five months too long in the man's estimation.

His concentration on the wall outside was broken when he heard his name come from behind him. He turned to see a deputy standing on the other side of the bars, staring at him.

"Tyler. You have a visitor," the man barked for a second time.

Without a word in response, Alvin hopped down off the top bunk. His feet hit the floor with a thud. He made his way down the center aisle of the barracks, dodging inmates sweeping the floor. As he approached the bars, he asked, "who is it? Family? Ain't no damn family come to see me in five months."

"Naw. Some FBI guy says you have information about a bolita game." The deputy inserted his skeleton key in the door. He turned it and the locking mechanism opened with a clank.

Without a word in response, Tyler followed the deputy out of the exterior barracks and into the main jail complex. The two were connected by a long hallway. A slight incline spoke to the fact the main structure had been erected upon a more substantial foundation.

Two large metal doors with windows in the upper half separated the hallway from the main building. Mesh wiring was blown into the panes, deterring potentially violent entrances and exits. As the two approached the doors the deputy reached down and pushed the horizontal bar that released the lock. He walked through the open entry and held the door open for Tyler to follow.

Once inside, the deputy held his open palm against the prisoner's chest and stopped him. Reaching for the wall next to the door frame, the officer removed a set of chains from which a pair of handcuffs dangled. He wrapped the chain around Tyler's waist and secured the handcuffs to the man's wrists. "Let's go."

The two continued advancing toward an interrogation room at the far end of the hallway. As they approached the door, the deputy opened it forcefully and without hesitation.
There was a man wearing a suit sitting at the table. He calmly looked at the two and said not a word.

The deputy pushed Tyler inside the room, backed away, and closed the door, isolating the two men.

Tyler recognized the man as one of the four who brought him to the FBI offices the day before. The man was large, muscular, and intimidating. More than adequate biceps and triceps stretched suit fabric to its maximum. Hoover liked strong, virile, young men in his agency. Nothing occupied the table's surface but the man's forearms and clasped hands. No notes would document their meeting.

Tyler took the chair on the opposite side of the table and sat meekly looking at the man who potentially controlled his future. He waited patiently for the G-Man to offer whatever reason he had for calling the meeting.

"The director has decided to honor your request."

"What request was that?" Tyler asked.

Not wishing to verbalize goals, the agent spoke only to the means that would lead to an acceptable end for all parties involved. "How many prisoners are there in your barracks?"

"Twenty-seven." Tyler paused and offered a complaint. "The place was only built for twenty. They've got us in there like animals."

The nameless G-Man didn't care. "Is Preston McDonald in there with you?"

Tyler visualized all the faces in the room that occupied his imagination. He slowly shook his head. "I don't know. There's some guy called P-Mac."

The agent scratched his right eyebrow and flashed a disgusted glance at the prisoner. "Make sure that's him. He needs to be the ringleader. Nothing, and I mean nothing can speak to you being the focus of this action."

Tyler nodded his understanding.

The agent reached with his right hand into his left, inside jacket pocket. Between his middle and forefinger was a loop of fishing line. It was ten feet in length and thin, only a four-pound test. He placed it on the table in front of him and slid it across to Tyler.

The prisoner quickly retrieved it and secured it in his waistband. "What's dis fo'?"

"Make sure you give that to Preston McDonald."

Tyler nodded.

"What time do they let you guys into the exercise yard?"

"Right afta breakfas'. Between nine and ten o'clock. They feed us late. The white prisoners get to eat first."

"Okay. At 9:25 have Preston take this fishing line over to the southwest corner of the wall. There will be a buddy of his on the other side with a hacksaw blade. Have Preston McDonald," the man emphasized the name again to demonstrate his importance to the plan, "cast this line over the wall. His buddy will attach the blade. He can pull it over the wall and shove it down his pants."

"Den what?"

"Then you hack your way out of those barred windows tomorrow night." The agent thought for a moment. "And not that I need to say this, but make sure it's a window that looks onto the street."

"Dat's it?"

"No. Not even close. You need to make sure you get as many of the guys in the barracks to go with you two."

"Why?"

"Because we need as many black guys loose as possible. We need the search party to be herding cats. It'll create a great deal of confusion as to your true whereabouts."

Tyler nodded satisfactorily, as a smile grew on his face.

"One more thing," the agent insisted. "You have to make sure that Loman Rivers is in the group that escapes."

"Why's dat?"

"He's in on federal charges. That'll open the escape to a federal issue, and I can then lead the task force, and direct them away from your true location."

There was an intensity emanating from the smile on Tyler's face. No one in his life ever recognized innate potential to lead a successful life. Greater successes as a criminal were brought forth by opportunities provided by law enforcement.

20

April 8, 1937. Two days after Clyde Hysler had been sentenced to death. Alvin Tyler sat atop his bunk in the barracks. It was late in the evening and bunkmates were long since asleep. The plan had been communicated to all twenty-seven inmates. Only seventeen agreed to the escape, including Rivers and McDonald. The prisoner hoped beyond hope the G-man's intentions were pure. He'd heard of mass escapes being orchestrated in order to justify the mass murder of society's undesirables.

Death was the sentence awaiting the young man: levied by the citizens of the community in which he purposefully murdered innocence. His white coconspirator had the economic means to challenge the verdict. Tyler didn't.

Of the three men involved in the murder of John and Mayme Surrency, only one had the ear of the F.B.I. The relationship had been developed over years. Petty crimes were allowed to be committed by the man for self-preservation. His penchant for destruction made him the ultimate assassin employed by a government determined to eliminate those who pressed for individual freedoms. Drugs and gambling were not the sole arena in which the mafia operated. An institution in control of a standing army possessed the ability to eliminate competition with little resistance. Men who dealt in violence understood the unequal distribution of strength.

Tyler was astute enough to have kept records of men he'd dealt with over the prior decade. Crimes had been committed in the name of centralizing control. It was leverage that saved his life. Genius was the government's ability to bring three men together and cast a shadow on the true ringleader. The other two men were expendable and made to tread the waters of the legal system on their own.

Divergent paths separated the two assailants. Baker had been dealt a bad hand given socioeconomic circumstances. Petty crimes and bolita were a means of survival. When it came time to elevate to armed robbery, the man simply didn't have the stomach for it. He pled with Tyler to forget the whole affair; to drive away. That which he thought was a crime for a two-hundred-dollar payoff escalated to murder. He sat inside the barracks with Tyler and agreed to participate in the escape.

Clyde Hysler had the unfortunate luck of being born into a crime family. Murder of, and by, uncles had been a part of his consciousness from the earliest age of understanding. It was his lot in life. Boastful conversations across the dinner table spoke to unsolved deaths at the hands of family members. If it was not his DNA, his environment doomed him to death at the age of twenty-eight. Only twenty-two at the time of the crime, his brain had yet to fully mature into a man possessing critical thought. Conception of murder for hire beset the discernment of a five-year-old, shielding his eyes from the reality surrounding him. If no one witnessed him commit the crime, he could not be found guilty of the murders. He sat in the adjacent building inside a cell of his own, totally unaware of the plan to free the two men he hoped would eventually take the blame for his actions.

The FBI used the white man's family in a more discrete manner than that of Tyler. Connections between the government agency and high-level crime bosses created calls to action for lower-level lieutenants, like Clyde's father and uncles. The impetuous youth felt as though his value within their criminal organization was growing. Moving higher in the ranks could be the only result of the Surrency's execution. Conviction on both counts were devastating to the young man. Assurances were given by arrogant attorneys the verdicts, and most importantly, the sentence of death would be vacated upon appeal.

For all of the disadvantages in life experienced by all three men, Alvin Tyler's reality was most brutal. Generational anger was passed down within the family. Parents and grandparents told the young boy he'd never amount to anything. He was stupid and would never be successful in school. Beatings drew the soul away from connecting with the universe and doomed him to exist in a purely physical manner. It was in that which he excelled, and the FBI recognized it from an early age.

Agency apparatus was instrumental in building an off the books army of young men across the country, all while putting forth a public face as America's top cops. Men of questionable character ascended to lofty positions whereby control was centralized. The creation of desperation in underserved communities provided an unending army of willing participants. Subversive activities plagued humanity.

Prisoners were not allowed to have watches, nor clocks on the wall. Comfort of time was not a luxury allowed the dregs of society. Tyler peered through the barred window facing the exercise yard. It was a clear night, and the full moon was visible and low in the night's sky. At the time it reached its apex in the sky the prisoner would know the time to be near midnight. It was decided that would be the best time to begin working on removing the bars that stood between the seventeen and freedom.

Although he possessed leverage, he knew whatever life remained would be in service of the FBI. He was fully aware agents could murder him and cancel their contract. As long as he was willing to do their dirty work, he would be protected by elite law enforcement.

His life was certain to be slated for death. The state of Florida did not hesitate in carrying out the wishes of its citizens. Urgency dictated Tyler be freed sooner rather than later. Both he and Baker obtained a glimpse into their future that became all too real upon the conviction of the man who'd hired them to complete the task.

Hours passed. When the time was deemed optimal, Tyler jumped to the floor from his seated position at the edge of his bunk. Quietly, he walked about the floor, waking the other members of the seventeen.

In all the time he sat waiting to be freed, not once did he consider the lives of John and Mayme Surrency. Never once did he inquire of his handler as to the why. Future jobs completed on behalf of the agency were considered. Opportunities to prove value as he conceived were welcomed without question.

Men queued at the window farthest from the main building and closest to the street. One at a time, each possessed the saw. Short bursts of intense energy were spent sawing the basses of the bars where they met the window's lower ledge. When exhaustion slowed one man, the blade was handed to another. This activity was repeated until the bars no longer blocked their escape.

One-by-one the men crawled through the window and disappeared into the night. No one moved with any purpose other than seeking shadowy paths to freedom. Of the seventeen, only Tyler sought out a person who would aid his escape beyond the streets of Jacksonville.

Tyler jogged west on Bay Street away from the jail complex. The men he'd lived with for five months disappeared behind homes and ran into alley ways they knew well. His purpose was to seek the machine operated by his liberator. At the intersection of Liberty Street, he glanced south toward the Saint Johns River. A block down sat a black Ford sedan. The driver's side window was rolled down and cigarette smoke drifted from the opening.

The prisoner approached the vehicle cautiously. Sitting inside and expressionless was his handler. The savior of his human form, and the enemy of his soul, was there to salvage the physical manifestation of Alvin Tyler. Purely selfish reasons motivated all involved in criminal pursuits. Integrity is a trait devoid within the criminal consciousness.

"Come on, boy. Let's go."

"Where we goin'?"

"Horse farm in Ocala. You'll be safe there until we can decide what to do with you."

The driver snaked his way through the streets, surreptitiously moving toward the Saint Johns River Bridge. Moving across the river and then south progressed toward common goals, closer to safety and the longevity Tyler desired. Neither knew on that night, but Tyler would never be made to pay for his crimes. The man lived out his days in anonymity. No one knows whether he had a family. What was certain was he'd destroyed the foundation of a group of people who'd feel the effects of his crime for generations.

21

The morning was warm. Summers in Jacksonville offered no relief from Florida heat. Garland made his way from his parked car to the office he'd occupied for eight years. Beneath his suit coat, sweat made his skin clammy, and his shirt wet. Thoughts of Maine this time of year occupied his thoughts.

More than a year after the prosecution for the murders of John and Mayme Surrency, life for the state's attorney returned to prosecutions for crimes less heinous. The residents of Jacksonville held disregard for murders by and of men who engaged in illegal lifestyles. It was acceptable they eliminate one another. Pressure waned and he once again fell into a repetitive work-a-day existence.

He entered the building as he had done throughout his career. Familiar faces greeted him at the reception desk. Pleasantries were exchanged as was customary. Moving further into the first-floor atrium, Garland spied the elevator operator, and the two exchanged a smile. The operator stepped to the side of the open lift. He offered a welcoming gesture with a wave of his arm through the open doors. Garland shook his head and smiled politely. Pointing to the door of the stairwell, he preferred the alternative.

Once inside the stairwell the man of forty looked dauntingly at the steps. Determined, he ascended the first flight two at a time. He stopped on the landing between the first and second floors to catch his breath. His heart beat a little faster. He never recalled being so stressed. Athletic endeavors of youth yielded to all that was unhealthy for a man who pursued morality. Laughing at his aging body, the prosecutor chose to take the remaining steps one at a time.

Upon reaching the door to the second floor, he stopped and drew in several deep breaths in an attempt to regulate his heartbeat. Once he was able to breathe normally, he walked through the door, down the hallway, and into his office.

Upon entering he saw the pretty Holli Goldman. She'd been his faithful assistant the entire time he occupied the office. Rare was the occasion he arrived before she did. As he moved past her, they exchanged their usual morning greetings. He looked beyond her pleasing countenance and absorbed the energy of her soul. She was someone who held his complete trust.

She called to him as he opened his door and stepped into his office. "Mr. Headley."

He stepped back into the outer office. "Yes?"

His assistant pointed toward the guest seating area he'd just passed without awareness. "Miss Slater is here to see you."

Garland glanced over to his visitor and smiled at the familiar face. "Hello, Margaret. What brings you here?"

The woman stood and walked toward the man. "I hoped you could spare a few minutes for me?"

"Of course." He waved her into his office with the hand unladen by his ever-present briefcase.

The two walked inside, and Margaret took an immediate left turn toward the fireplace and sitting area. Garland watched as she sat on the couch with her back to the door. The prosecutor walked to his desk and sat his case down atop it before joining the woman.

Once settled he looked at his visitor and asked, "so, what brings you here today?"

She smiled. "I've got good news, and bad. Which do you want first?"

Garland breathed deeply. "Gimme the bad."

Without hesitation she launched into the reason for her visit. "I wanted to let you know that I will be changing jobs. I will be at the Internal Revenue Service from now on."

It was a curious notion, coming to his office for a seemingly benign change of circumstances. He knew there must be something more compelling her visit. "Well, I wish you much success."

She smiled and nodded her appreciation.

When she did not respond further, he exercised the elephant in the room. "What precipitated the move?"

"I'm afraid I angered J. Edgar."

"How?"

"Incessant questioning of the bureau's stance on the Surrency murders."

"What kind of questions were you asking?"

"I looked at the facts of the case with a critical eye. I'd swear Tyler was the one in control of John and Mayme's fate. He seemed to manipulate the other two. I asked if he was one of our assets?"

"You mean confidential informant?"

The woman shook her head. "No. I believe we employ assets to commit crimes to further the need for our services ... to justify the FBI's existence."

"Are you serious? They would do that?"

The woman nodded. "Yes. Ask yourself, who solved the murders?"

"Sheriff Swift and his deputies. Those men worked tirelessly to make sure these men were brought to justice."

"Exactly. There really is no need for law enforcement beyond local authorities. There are good men and women who are more than capable of protecting communities across the country." She paused. "I'm certain we had something to do with Tyler's escape two days after Hysler's death sentence for Mayme's murder."

Garland took a moment to digest the gravity of his friend's assertions. "Do you think they'd ever increase the scale of crimes?"

"In order to gain greater control over the country, most definitely."

The prosecutor had difficulty comprehending the scale of crimes to which his friend feared a so-called benevolent organization would commit. Corruption counted on that kind of innocence. People unable to assimilate evil won't believe it exists. He shook his head. "I'm … I just don't know."

Without hesitation, Margaret continued. "Are you familiar with General Smedley Butler's testimony before congress."

Cracked pieces of a mosaic began to form a mental picture. The general's declaration was five years earlier, in 1933. Garland recalled dismissing it as outlandish. His experiences since that time strengthened the words of the respected military man. Wishing to hear all Miss Slater had to say, he feigned ignorance. "It seems I recall something about that, but what did he say?"

Without hesitation, she launched into her diatribe. "He testified he'd been approached by a consortium of businessmen who asked for his help overthrowing FDR's government. He was so well-respected among the troops. He fought for back-pay promised soldiers by the government, but never paid. These fascists thought they had a willing army, and a leader of those men who could easily capture the country for themselves." She shook her head. "I never knew possessing a long-term perspective could bring such clarity. Do you recall one of our earlier meetings before the trial?"

Garland nodded.

"I told you we had changed from the Bureau of Investigation to the Federal Bureau of Investigation?"

He nodded, once again.

"That was also 1933. The FBI was transferred to a corporation owned not by the United States but private interests. The same year these *businessmen* approached Smedley Butler." She looked Garland squarely in the eyes. "There are no coincidences, my friend." Her stare shifted to the empty fireplace. "God only knows what I'll learn about the IRS."

Questions remained in the prosecutor's mind. He attempted to shift her away from her digression, and back onto the subject of her change. "I still don't understand the need to move you to the IRS?"

"There really is no need for the change. These are my personal opinions, but they are based on working knowledge of the local office. I think Hoover became frustrated that local law enforcement and politicians were incorruptible."

"So, they moved you to the IRS?"

She shook her head. "The local office is no longer a field office. All management duties have been shifted to the Miami office. Talk about a banana republic." She smiled. "Anyway, the office here will hold nothing more than a few field agents. It seems Sheriff Swift's philosophy that there will always be a demand for liquor and prostitutes was spot on. Keep the activities regulated locally, and don't let them get out of hand. Allow your men to take a few kickbacks to supplement their income, but draw the line when crime becomes organized beyond individual transactions."

"Wow," he thought. "It all makes sense."

"Garland, ten years ago, if I'd heard myself say these words, I'd have said I lost the plot. Called myself crazy. It's interesting the clarity that comes with an elongated and detailed timeline of one's life." She paused. "Plus, there are just too many hushed conversations around the office."

"Clarity is the perfect word, but the implications are scary as hell."

Margaret brought the reason for her visit to fruition. "I just want you to be careful. Something tells me this ordeal with

John and Mayme isn't done."

"How so?"

"Hysler will appeal this all the way to the Florida Supreme Court ... the United States Supreme Court, if necessary. The family has plenty of money from their ill-gotten gains, but I'm afraid they have funding sources from within our government who have a vested interest in making sure crime families maintain control across generations. It keeps citizens in fear ... and in need of some greater power for protection. When guys like Clyde and Tyler get caught, it provides plausible deniability."

Garland thought for a moment. "I guess the best we can hope for is they'll sacrifice the Clyde pawn, and it will all be over?"

"Maybe, but I wouldn't count on it. To the contrary, what I would worry about most if I were you is that stories will change. Witnesses will die unexpectedly. That's just how these people work. Total disregard for life ... including yours and mine."

Garland sat silently grasping the enormity of her words. For a man who'd achieved the pinnacle of prosecutorial office for the county, he felt as though life was closing in on him. Seeking to hear positive news, he asked about Margaret's second reason for her visit. "You mentioned some good news?"

"Oh yes. It seems there's a girl in our office that has requested a formal introduction."

A handsome, successful state's attorney was in demand, and Miss Slater's request did not come as a surprise. "What is your assessment of this young lady?"

Slater nodded her head in an unconvincing side-to-side manner. "She's smart. She nice. She's a hard worker."

Garland smiled. "Nice? Smart? Hard worker? Sounds like a German Shepherd."

"Oh, she's far from a German Shepherd." Margaret tilted her head to the right. "If I'm not mistaken, I think she said she met you briefly."

The prosecutor scanned his memory for the comings and goings in his recent life. "I just don't know, Margaret. Who is it?"

"Her name is Nhi Kurosawa."

Garland sat up straight. "Nhi?"

"Yes."

Excitement bubbled like magma within the deepest recesses of his soul. He couldn't allow his guest to see the lava burst forth from his countenance. Rendered incapable of speech until his soul was calmed, he disguised excitement with a half-hearted smile and a nod of his head.

"Are you acceptable to an introduction?"

He nodded.

"I'm not sure if you understand, but given the fact that Nhi is Japanese, her father had to give permission for the meeting."

He nodded.

"Are you okay?"

He nodded.

For all of his bravado, it became clear to his visitor how excited he was to receive the request. Margaret retrieved a slip of paper from her pocketbook and slid it across the table toward her host. "Here's the address. Be there Sunday at three o'clock. And whatever you do, don't be late."

Garland was finally able to gather himself. "You said Kurosawa?"

"Yes."

"Her father is the rich industrialist, Niko Kurosawa?"

"Yes."

"We've actually met briefly, twice."

"Well … apparently you made a good impression on them both. I can't impress on you enough the Japanese take these meetings very seriously. Your days of twenty-three skidoo are over."

"A union between a man and a woman should be taken seriously. And I assure you I am serious … and honorable in my intentions."

Margaret stood and walked to the office door. "I'll deliver your acceptance to Nhi." The woman reached down and opened the door. Just before exiting, she felt compelled to turn and offer one last thought. She smiled. "I think Nhi will be as excited as you are."

Garland offered only a smile in response. After closing the door behind his guest, he walked to his desk, sat with his hands folded behind his head, and smiled like the proverbial Cheshire cat. His career had been filled with death and ending the activities of rogue humans. For the first time he envisioned an eternal existence. Nhi possessed an energy unlike any woman he'd met. It was calm. It was settled in its human form. The man knew the universe would never allow such beauty to be extinguished. She was the first who stoked his conception of eternity. Thoughts of John and Mayme entered his mind. He became convinced their souls were around to see how tirelessly he worked on their behalf. At that moment, avenging deaths became secondary to freeing earthly burdens. Never had he peered beyond the outcome of a trial. He'd always desired a role as advocate for victims. The mere mention of Nhi's name provided the man a conception of a wider universe, and better, eternal circumstances for the victims of the most heinous crime in Jacksonville's history.

22

September 26, 1937. Sheriff Swift sat at his desk. Work had once again become innocuous. The most infamous murders in Jacksonville's history had been solved and successfully prosecuted by his friend, Garland Headley.

Domestic disturbances, drunken brawls, and people accused of stealing chickens dominated the reports on his desk. Focused discernment was applied to each account he read. Outside influences would be dealt with harshly, especially those involving prostitution and illegal hooch. Those had been the vices focused on by national crime organizations. Rex lived the effects of centralized control on lives of young men who fought in the war to end all wars. He'd left many friends on the battlefield and returned home. For the sake of Jacksonville and its residents, this was a hill on which he was prepared to die.

A knock sounded at his door. He knew it to be one of his deputies. Everyone else was made to enter through his secretary. "Come in."

In walked Deputy Peter McLaurin. He held his cap in his hand and fidgeted nervously.

"Well, what is it?" the sheriff pressed.

The deputy closed his eyes and shook his head. "They killed John B."

"Hysler?"

"Yes, sir."

"Who?"

"Those damned … I mean those dry agents?"

"Federal guys?"

"Uh huh."

"Shit," the sheriff exclaimed as he looked around his office for answers.

"He'd gone down to Mineral City to pick up a load of hooch. They surrounded him on the Saint Johns River Bridge and shot him dead."

"For carryin' a load of hooch? That's it?"

"Yes, sir."

The sheriff spoke rhetorically and to the air around him. "I know that family's never up to any good, but that's no reason to kill a man … or even take a shot at him."

"That's that boy's uncle, ain't it?"

The sheriff knew his deputy was referring to Clyde Hysler. "Yeah. That family's got murderous tendencies. They've proven that over the years, but John B? No way. God, I wish they'd let us take the lead on local matters."

The two men sat silently, pondering the implications. Rex broke the silence between them. "That's it?"

"Yes, sir."

"Make sure that report gets to me as soon as it is completed."

"But that's their report. None of our guys were there."

Irritated, the sheriff had to remind the young deputy of his standing. "I am the highest-ranking constitutional officer in Duval County. Go over there and get the report when it's finished and bring it to me."

The deputy exited the office without a word. Sheriff Swift resumed the task of scanning reports seeking reasons for concern above basic facts of each incident. Hours passed. An occasional trip to the kitchen to fetch a cup of coffee broke the monotony.

At 3:38 P.M. the sheriff's intercom sparked to life. His secretary announced the presence of a man called Riley Jasperson. "Who's that?"

"Says he has information from the Fruit Grower's Express."

"Send him in."

The door opened to reveal an older black man wearing bib overalls. His hairline was receding, and his beard was completely gray and offered a stark contrast to his dark skin. He held his hat in his hand and stood just inside the door awaiting permission to proceed further.

The sheriff waved him inside. "Come on in. Have a seat."

The man moved silently to one of the chairs in front of the sheriff's desk and sat down without a word spoken.

"You work at the Grower's Express?"

"Yessa."

"What can I help you with?"

"Nossa. It's what I got to help you."

Rex smiled and raised his eyebrows in an accepting manner. "I'm listening."

"It's them boys what done killed Mr. John and Miss Mayme."

"The Surrencys?"

"Yessa."

"We've convicted two of the three involved."

"Nossa. It's not about the boys that killed 'em. It's the why."

The sheriff sat back in his chair and became somewhat perturbed. "Did you speak to our deputies when they came to the warehouse to investigate?"

"Yessa."

"And you didn't tell them what you're about to tell me."

The man shook his head, embarrassedly. "Nossa."

"Why not?"

"Well, because I was afraid it might make Mr. John and Miss Mayme look bad."

The sheriff sat forward once again, resting his forearms on the edge of the desk in front of him. "And what might that be?"

"You see … miss Mayme had the troubles with the laudanum. Mr. John was like a hawk around her. He loved his wife." A tear welled on the lower eye lids of the man. "Seems Mr. John cared for all of us." He paused. "That Hysler boy … he come 'round the warehouse tryin' to get miss Mayme some heroin."

"That's in the report, Mr. Jasperson."

"But what nobody told you was 'dat he wanted all the men at the warehouse to get addicted to that drug. Mr. John didn't beat the piss out 'dat Hysler boy to protect his wife. He wanted to protect all of us."

Sheriff Swift glared through his office window, onto the parking lot filled with cars. Without removing his stare, or looking at his visitor, the sheriff ended the meeting. "Thank you, Mr. Jasperson."

The old man stood and exited the office as silently as he'd entered.

Two facts entered the man's consciousness that day, and neither came from an official report. John B. had been killed by federal agents, and Clyde had been attempting to create a larger market for heroin. Seemingly unrelated events made perfect sense to the skeptical law enforcement officer. John B. would have known what his nephew was attempting. In all of his run-ins with the law the elder Hysler never ventured beyond cheap, illegal, booze. Maybe he'd attempted to stop his nephew from making a mistake? Maybe the feds felt as though the man knew too much and needed to be eliminated. Regardless, anecdotal evidence continued to speak of the fruitful association between federal law enforcement and organized crime.

23

Sheriff Swift sat at the sofa in Garland Headley's office. Across the coffee table the state's attorney stared back at the man. The date was July 21, 1938. The fireplace adjacent the seating area had long lay dormant. Ash was cleared from its box. The sun's path across the sky had begun its annual descent into the southern hemisphere. Regardless of the retreat, effects of the Florida summer were full. The attorney's jacket found its usual space on the hall-tree next to his office door. Decorum dictated the sheriff wear his as a visitor. Etiquette was quickly dispensed in a time without air-conditioned rooms. Both men were clad in sweat-stained shirts and the sheriff's jacket was cast across the back of the sofa next to him.

Headley's back was to the exterior wall and the bank of windows that consumed it. Sheriff Swift stared past the couch occupied by the prosecutor at the glare bursting through glass panes. Waves of heat rolled across the officer's face and emanated in his psyche. People lived in Florida for the winters. Summers were unbearable in a time without convenience.

For the man who grew up in nearby Camden County, Georgia, he understood one must take the good with the bad. Northern states enjoyed pleasant summers but must deal with harsh winters. Service in World War I offered the opportunity to meet soldiers from all over Europe. Darren McCready was a Scottish fighter who crossed paths with Rex after the Battle of Somme. Inquiring of living conditions in Scotland, the man remarked in his brogue laden speech, "most of the time it's very pleasant, but winters are fucking miserable." That sentiment reflected the man's circumstance in the middle of a Florida July.

Pleasantries had been exchanged by the men, and they waited. Their forthcoming guest was Noble Enge, the son-in-law of the Surrencys. Convictions of all men involved in the Surrency's murder aged by over a year. He'd run for county commission during the early part of the prior decade and lost in the primary. He was a man of integrity at a time when money flowed freely and intoxicated the populace. Prohibition had done nothing to quell demand for spirits. Citizens were numbed by physical pleasures. The two men seated in the office of the state's attorney knew the hangover could prove deadly to the town on the verge of success.

Although the Sheriff allowed his deputies to take a cut from the local prostitution and bootleg rings, he looked upon vices as biblical. As long as humans walked the earth, immorality found its way into communities. Hell bent on not allowing local thieves to take over, all were kept well in check by the Duval Sheriff's office. Equally determined was the man to keep organized crime from taking over. A student of history, the man knew of George Washington's declaration that the United States should engage in no foreign entanglements. Fervor had been whipped up by the federal government in order to garner support for World War I. The man witnessed some of the vilest acts humans exacted on one another, and he'd been complicit.

Logic employed by the aging man conceived the dynamics of reaching into European countries and extracting life and value. He understood to protect his community he must defend it from outside forces. Octopus tentacles extracted without threat to the central body. If one were lopped off by local law enforcement, a new apparatus would grow and replace the old.

Garland instructed his assistant to show Mr. Enge into the office upon arrival, which she did. The door to the office opened. Miss Goldman walked into the room and glanced toward the attorney's desk. Seeing it had been vacated, she peered around the edge of the door and spied the two men seated on the sofas. From behind her appeared Mr. Enge, hat in hand.

Sheriff Swift was motivated to stand when he saw the welcoming smile of his counterpart, as he stood.

"Come in, Mr. Enge," the man greeted, and waved him to the comfort of their sitting area.

Mr. Enge's face was round and pleasant. His countenance shined with a genuine smile. A man without stain on his conscience was free of consternation when meeting the highest law officials in the county.

The Norwegian sat next to the attorney. He preferred his back to the wall, and a clear vision of entry into the room. Involvement in politics taught the man there was an element in town who would harm anyone who hindered profits. Threats had been made against his life over a decade ago, and memories were indelibly stained and dictated actions. Thoughts concerning the motivation for his in-law's deaths were kept to himself. His wife would never know his suspicion of the people with whom her parents had been involved.

Once all three men settled into their seats, the visitor smiled once again, and looked his hosts in their eyes. He nodded acceptance of their association.

Laden by a thick Norwegian accent, the visitor inquired, "what can I do for you gentlemen?"

The prosecutor and the sheriff glanced at one another, unsure of who should take the lead. Garland nodded and winked. "Mr. Enge, we've invited you here today to ask you to become more involved in our community. Jacksonville now has over a hundred thousand residents, and I certainly would not be surprised if it eclipsed a quarter million by the turn of the next century."

The Norwegian nodded, smiled, and glanced between the two men. Congeniality was effervescent. "How can I help you gentlemen?"

Sheriff Swift leaned forward and sat at the edge of the sofa. "You ran for county commission in '22. We would like you to run again."

The visitor sat back and settled into his seat. Relief permeated his psyche at the understanding of the meeting's purpose. "Gentlemen, I lost the primary. The good people of Duval County don't want a man like me holding office."

"But you're sixteen years wiser," Garland interjected.

The Norwegian shook his head. "But the challenges I would face have only gotten stronger. I'm not a fighter."

Sheriff Swift shook his head vigorously. "You won't have to fight. I'll be here for that."

The ever-present smile persisted, although the man's inner voice was diametrically opposed to the men's proposal. "Sheriff, you have done a good job for our county since you were first elected five years ago. But you have the skills, and the temperament to affect change. I don't."

Garland shifted his body to face the man on the sofa next to him. "Mr. Enge, you have the skills necessary for what we're attempting to accomplish in the community. With you on the county commission, and with your profile in the community, we can direct funds where they are necessary to fight these outside influences." He paused and glanced at the sheriff, unsure of whether he should mention the Surrencys. He did. "And ... with the fact that your in-laws were murdered you have an awareness of and have felt the sting of crime."

The pleasant smile never left the man's face. Without answering immediately, he reached inside his jacket. From his shirt pocket he retrieved a yellowed bit of newspaper that was folded in half. He handed it to the prosecutor. Garland extended the clipping from its fold and read the words and digested the meaning of the picture. In his hand was a political cartoon published in the Florida Metropolis on October 15, 1915. It depicted a man in a suit and hat walking on a sidewalk around the corner of a building. He is whistling, seemingly without a care in the world. Waiting around the corner, behind the edge of a building, are all manner of the local criminal element. Wielding bricks, clubs, knives, spears, hoes, and even a lady dressed in proper Victorian style, holding an umbrella ready to strike. The criminal population lay in wait to cause harm to the man. Across the top the caption read, "GETTING EVEN WITH ENGE THE ARTIST."

THE FLORIDA METROPOLIS -- October 15, 1915

Garland understood the gravity of their request of Mr. Enge. He silently handed the clipping across the coffee table to Sheriff Swift.

As the sheriff digested the meaning of the cartoon, their guest continued. "The Enge in that cartoon is my brother Axle. He also ran for County Commission. When I ran, I was much younger. I knew my brother, older than myself, hadn't campaigned properly. He was out of touch with the community. I knew I could do much better." He glanced between the two again. "My experience was the same."

Never one to relent completely, Garland mentioned, "today is the 21st. In order to run you must file by the 25th. Would you at least consider our proposal?"

The Norwegian drew in and exhaled a deep breath. "You give me four days?"

Again, the sheriff and prosecutor looked to one another.

Garland looked at Noble. "That's all the time we have left for this cycle."

The Norwegian dropped his head. Almost as if summoning God through prayer, he sat motionless for nearly a minute. It was his turn to draw in and exhale a deep breath. The visitor became alert, looked up at his two hosts. Quick, sharp nods of his head affirmed his participation. "I'll do it."

24

Garland drove his 1936 Buick Series 40 Drophead Coupe down Riverside Avenue. Taking a left on Osceola Street he drove a tenth of a mile until the forced left onto River Boulevard. He knew the house well but drove slowly as if needing to seek out his destination. He attempted to calm his nerves by telling himself they asked for the introduction. Nothing seemed to help a man who appreciated the importance of this first meeting with Nhi's family.

He slowed the vehicle and veered toward the curb next to the seawall that protected the area from surging water levels. He sat in his car and removed his pocket watch. It was 2:55 PM. He knew being early was just as disrespectful as being late. Nervously, he wound the stem of his watch until it wouldn't wind further. He kept attempting to turn it motivated by anxiety, until his conscious mind became aware of potential damage to the timepiece.

Looking again at the watch face. 2:56 PM. He shifted his gaze to the wooden dock that extended into the river to his right. At its end was moored a wooden seventeen-foot Chris Craft Deluxe Runabout. Garland sat staring out over the water, imagining he and Nhi taking weekend pleasure trips on the boat. He was shaken back into reality when he checked his watch. It was 2:59 PM. The top of the hour approached quickly.

Hurriedly, he emerged from his car and walked toward the grand home. It was built from buff-colored brick in an eclectic style that reflected Colonial Revival. The young man moved down the sidewalk. Approaching the home, he took in the grandeur of the French tiled roof, and worried the family watched from the windows. Coming to a stop in front of the door, he saw several pairs of shoes of varying sizes placed on the patio beside the entry. Alternating hands with which he held flowers, he removed his shoes and placed them neatly next to the others. Fear gripped him as he wondered if visitors should place their shoes on the opposite side of the doorway.

Standing in front of the door, almost ready to ring the bell, he looked down at his stocking feet. "Yes. I should take off my socks too." Quickly he removed his socks, placing each inside the respective shoe that originally covered them.

Finally, he stood as prepared as he'd ever be to meet a young woman who'd dipped into and out of his consciousness for years. He rang the bell and waited.

When the door opened, he saw the man he'd met a few times over the years. "Hello. I am Niko Kurosawa," and then bowed.

Garland felt obligated to return the gesture. He held his hand out. "I'm Garland Headley."

"Yes," the old man replied as he shook the hand of his visitor.

Looking beyond the man standing in his doorway, Niko spied the car on the street. "I see your car is a couple years old." He nodded. "Practical. Not at all ostentatious."

Garland felt that could be a good sign.

The old man continued. "But I see it is a coupe. Not conducive for family."

Oof. The first emotional dagger plunged into his psyche. Garland wished to advance the conversation. "I'm not sure if you recall, but we've met a couple times over the years."

"Yes. I am aware." The old man walked inside the house, and Garland followed. "I have admired the manner in which you pursue justice. You are good for our community."

"Thank you, sir. That means a lot."

The two men walked together fifty feet down a hallway. Stopping in front of pocket doors with cherry blossoms painted on the upper glassed portion. The windows were opaque, and Garland could only imagine what awaited inside. Mr. Kurosawa smiled at his visitor and slid the doors apart.

Without advancing into the room, Garland peered inside to assess the situation. There were three women seated around a table whose surface was not twelve inches off the floor. Cushions provided relief from hardwood floors. Nhi sat on the far side and smiled when she saw Garland.

At the left end of the table sat an older woman that appeared to be Nhi's mother. An even older woman with gray hair sat with her back to the door. "It must be her grandmother. I can do this," Garland thought.

There were only two seats available for the men. One at the right end of the table and one next to the woman he hoped to court. Fear rattled his soul as he froze, not knowing which seat was traditionally meant for him.

Mr. Kurosawa entered the room and led his visitor. The old man held his hand out, offering the seat next to his daughter for Garland. "You will sit next to Nhi."

Without a word, Garland moved around the table and dropped to his knees next to the beautiful young girl. All three women were dressed in traditional kimonos, complete with obi. The stitching on each was unique to the woman. The American noticed Nhi's showed a scene of a boat on a river with cherry blossoms gracing a tree on the riverbank. He had no idea what message it was meant to convey.

Taking the lead from Nhi, Garland sat on his knees with his legs tucked beneath him. Mr. Kurosawa smiled and cleared his throat. "Men sit on their bottoms with their legs folded, like I am. Women sit like that in case they need to stand quickly to serve the men."

The second emotional strike shuttered his soul. Looking around the table he felt out of place. All were dressed in traditional Japanese clothes. He'd worn his most expensive

Brooks Brothers suit, but it did nothing to fend off feelings of inadequacy.

He so wanted to be accepted he rushed to utter the only Japanese word he knew. Its meaning was ascertained with the help of Jay and Tammy, friends at Jacksonville's Public Library. It was an attempt to assimilate his feelings for Niko's daughter. "I have a lot of Kokohaku for Nhi."

The old man burst into laughter. It was not traditional for an elder to show such emotion, but the man had lived and prospered in the United States long enough to express joviality. "I appreciate your attempt to embrace our culture." His next gesture, reaching out and grabbing the arm of his guest in comfort, was also not very Japanese. "How about we simply talk. Let's get to know one another."

25

Sunday, July 24, 1938, the Enge family returned from church. Ted, Bess, and Carol were in the backyard playing. Still in their church clothes, the ire of Miriam was palpable as she commanded them all to their rooms to change into something more appropriate. Six-month-old Kathy lay in her rolling bassinet in the kitchen as her mother prepared lunch. The morning sermon exhausted the infant, and she napped. Sweaty hair stuck to her still forming cranium. Her cheeks were rosy in the summer heat.

Arlington was a small, tightly knit community south of Jacksonville. The home in the first block of Windermere Drive sat adjacent to one occupied by Noble's parents. Father and son hunted together regularly. Keeping with Norwegian traditions, the artist passed along his skills in the kitchen to his wife. A quick study, she embraced the role of meal provider for the extended family on Sundays.

Noble sat in his favorite leather club chair in the family room. Cursorily reading the Times Union, his thoughts centered around the past week as well as that which lay ahead. As with most during the great depression, business bumped along the bottom and people struggled to tread financial waters. Glimmers of economic hope were apparent, and the man had a lot to look forward to regarding his young family.

There was a great deal of satisfaction gleaned from his station in life. The only real setback had been Ted's polio. The young man proved hearty and resilient. Shaking away the effects of an underdeveloped limb, he trained his body to operate along a different center of gravity. Arms were stronger than most and operated interchangeably as a second leg when necessary. Skills became so acute he would compete and win many pommel horse competitions as a young adult at the University of Florida.

The father's artistic mind held detailed visions of all of his children. Their importance to him could not be overstated. In times of reflection, he envisioned their growth into adulthood. With the exception of Kathy, each of the children took to the Norwegian language. Nightly fairy tales were read and spoken in his native tongue. Carol would lay next to her father. His arm wrapped around her, holding her tightly to his body. She pointed out pictured characters when she recognized names, and then looked to her father's face for approval. His smile meant everything to her.

Lunch was called and the family gathered around the long dining room table. Kathy was removed from her bassinet and placed in a highchair at the corner of the table next to her father. He patiently fed her pureed beets, carrots, and peas. Intermittently he took bites of the duck Miriam prepared for the Sunday feast. It was a fowl harvested on one of the many hunting trips taken with his father.

Ted sat at the table with one foot on the floor and his knee planted firmly in his seat. The twelve-year-old boy had many pressing issues and could not be bothered with a meal. Carol and Bess talked amongst themselves incessantly. Noble and Miriam exchanged smiles consumed by satisfaction toward their beautiful family.

Money was manipulated by a central authority. Its movement ebbed and flowed at the whims of men who created the mechanism at nearby Jekyll Island. Not without struggle, the Enges survived the Great Depression. No matter the financial status of the family, no one would ever be able to take from them the love shared amongst the six.

Play-clothes were donned before the meal at the behest of their mother. After obtaining permission from their parents to be excused, the three older children ran through the house and into the backyard to expel as much energy as possible. Days were long and offered plenty of time for children's recreation.

The family had a small garden in the backyard as well as a chicken coop. Many hens produced eggs regularly. On days the family couldn't consume all that was produced, Miriam took the excess to market for sale.

After lunch, Kathy was placed in a crib in the family room. The baby was just out of sight on the other side of the wall from the kitchen, where Miriam and Noble cleaned and dried dishes. Actively jumping, and babbling incessantly, the couple shared another smile at their youngest's determination to have herself heard.

The afternoon progressed as most other Sundays. Adults settled into that which passed time. Noble sat in his chair looking over the paperwork he was to file at the Supervisor of Elections office the following morning. It was tedious, but the man thrived on attention to detail.

As the afternoon progressed, impromptu yet regular Sunday naps consumed the consciousnesses of husband and wife. Manifesting from weekly exhaustion the couple found themselves fast asleep in their respective chairs in the family room. Kathy peered at her sleeping parents from her crib and instinctively knew not to call for either. Contently, she sat down in her crib and played with that which surrounded her. She was a peaceful child.

Only the sound of the wooden screened door slamming against its frame woke the sleeping couple. Groggily, they both sat up and assessed the surroundings of which they'd lost sight hours before.

Noble removed the watch from his vest pocket, looked at the time, and habitually wound its stem. Assessing the late hour, he looked through the living room window. His eyes fell onto Windermere Drive. The sun's effect had lost most of its influence and the sky reflected dark blue. Dinner consisted of leftovers from lunch and needed minimal preparation.

Struggling against the tranquilizer effects of such a long nap, the man stood and stretched all limbs to their extreme. He looked down at Miriam, and mentioned, "I'm going to feed the girls."

His wife sat forward in her chair and came to rest at its edge. Consumed in her attempt to wake herself, she did not respond to Noble as he made his way through the kitchen. Above the door was a twenty-gauge shotgun balanced on two nails. Without assessment of its need, the man reached up and grabbed the gun from its perch before exiting into the backyard. It was not beyond the realm of possibility to encounter a predator seeking an easy meal inside the coop.

Hens cackled loudly upon his approach to the coop. It was not unusual. The girls knew he was coming to fed them, and Noble thought nothing of the disturbance. Natural light quickly waned, and his eyes needed time to adjust. Familiarity with the layout compelled progress toward nightly tasks.

Holding the shotgun in his left hand, he reached toward the gate and turned its latch. Pushing forward into the pen, Noble switched the gun from his left hand to right, and then propped it against the door frame. He walked to the far side of the structure, followed, and surrounded by every chicken in the coop. "Good evening, girls. I know it's a little late, but I'll never forget about you ladies."

Noble lifted the lid on the wooden container that held bulk feed. An aluminum sifter whose handle and agitator had broken months earlier formed a second life as a ladle. Repurposing was the way of the depression. Scooping several loads of grain into pans on the ground the chickens quickly surrounded the circumferences of each feed-tray. Pecking incessantly, the chickens ignored the man.

Noble turned toward the gate and the vision of a man appeared from the darkness. The stranger held the father's shotgun in his left, and a pistol in his right. Curiosity crossed the man's countenance. He had no idea how to react.

The assailant flipped the barrel of the pistol sharply upward twice. Noble raised his arms into the air.

"Your brother Axle got the message, but I guess you didn't."

"I don't understand," Noble responded, innocently.

The stranger insisted, "we're not going to allow Swift and Headley to run this town."

"I'm just an artist."

"No. You're a politician, or at least you will be after tomorrow."

Noble dropped his hands and held them at his waist. He held his palms skyward and offered, "I won't file to run tomorrow. Simple as that."

The man shook his head. "Nope. That just won't get it. The same thing happened with your brother, and yet here we are again." He waved the barrel of his pistol toward the house. "If I let you live, it's my son that will have to deal with your crippled son in twenty years." He shook his head again. "This time we're playing for keeps. There's a message that needs to be sent, and it needs to be strong enough to last generations."

Noble drew in and exhaled a deep breath. He thought of his in-laws and the bravery shown by both. Resigned to his fate, he refused to grovel. It would only feed the ego of the murderer that stood before him.

Fortunate for the criminal, Noble brought his own gun to the chicken coop. A man shot by his own gun would appear as either a suicide or an accident. A perpetrator wouldn't be sought. The criminal placed the pistol in his pocket and drew a bead on the man with his own shotgun. The blast sent chickens scurrying.

Miriam stood over the stove and looked through the kitchen window into the backyard at the sound of the blast. "Noble must have seen a fox," she thought.

It would be an hour before the woman checked on her husband. She found his body inside the pen leaning against the door frame. The blood on his face and shirt dried crimson. His gun lay across his lap, confusing the presumption death was accidental or self-inflicted. Miriam let out a blood-curdling scream.

Her sister-in-law living next door heard the commotion and came running.

Both women knew Noble had been murdered. It was inconceivable a man who hunted regularly to provide for his family would experience a mishap with a firearm. Hardened by the depression, Miriam's thoughts turned immediately to her four children, for whom she was on her own to provide.

26

The prosecutor waited patiently in the outer vestibule of Sheriff Swift's office. News of Noble Enge's death came quickly and cut deeply. Both men felt culpable.

Uniformed deputies strolled in and out of the space as they made their way to and from patrol cars. Shifts changed and conversations centered around the night's activities. Full moons made for especially interesting evenings. Most crime in the growing city centered around human vice. Liquor violations and red-light disputes occupied much of the force's time. Even in a smallish city, dregs settled in and coalesced at its bottom.

Rare was the occasion of murder. At a time when frontiers yielded to burgeoning cities, those choosing to exist in urban areas embraced the notion of self-defense at all costs. Disputes among men were muted by the potential of either participant brandishing a deadly weapon. Natural was the tendency of urbanites to seek out that which offered immediate pleasure. No longer necessary was the need to prepare soil, plant, sew, and harvest. Every need was readily and immediately available. It was only the extent to which one yielded to desires that determined legality.

Garland and the sheriff understood God's timeline was eternal. Their jobs centered on rectifying those who fell from that timeline into a depraved existence. Random crimes were prosecuted in an assembly line format. Each a product of its own manifestation. Higher thinkers understood links between seemingly unrelated events. Existing on an eternal timeline proved difficult when life and career centered around flesh-driven circumstances. Garland appreciated the fact that Nhi had come into his life and offered a daily glimpse of the everlasting.

Merely three days after convincing Noble Enge to run for county commission the man was shot dead. The father of four was seen as an ally. A man who genuinely sought good for his city and its residents. Someone who viewed all humanity as brethren. The young family lost the soul of its father, and it was a void never filled.

The Sargent behind the desk called to Garland. "Mr. Headley, the sheriff is ready for you now."

"Thank you," he replied as he walked toward the door leading into the hallway. He strolled the long corridor to its end, where the sheriff's door was closed. He knocked, opened the door, and entered the office.

"Have a seat," the sheriff offered.

The prosecutor walked to one of the chairs in front of the sheriff's desk and sat without saying a word. The office was constructed of concrete block walls painted light green. Black and white photographs hung haphazardly and without uniformity. Strings anchored on each side of the frames were looped over nails, exposing trinities of support. Subject matter centered around his time in the War to End All Wars and presentations of appreciation from civic societies.

Never one to mince words, the sheriff assessed their situation. "We're in a raft of shit."

Garland nodded.

"To be completely honest with you, I had no idea how entrenched the mafia was in town. Five years in office has really opened my eyes."

The prosecutor shook his head. "I mentioned to you in '36 after the Surrency murders, when I found out Mayme's maiden name was Swearingen, that I felt the senator's death in Bartow might be connected. Now I'm certain all four deaths are related." He paused. "What that connection is, I don't know."

"I think you and I need to become joined at the hip. We've got to clean this town. I'll arrest and you prosecute."

Garland offered a muted rejection. "We need to focus on the connection between the murders of these family members."

"Where should we begin?"

"At the Surrencys funeral, a law school buddy of mine who is now the state's attorney in the Polk County district attended."

"He came all the way from Bartow for a funeral?"

Garland nodded. "He brought with him a handful of mugshots of men who worked for both Santo Trafficante and Ignacio Antinori. Damned if there was not a representative of each organization in attendance."

Sheriff Swift sat forward and began rifling through reports in his inbox. "Seems there was some mention of those two," he paused as he retrieved the document for which he searched. "Yep. Here it is. A statewide bulletin from the State Police. Those two organizations have been rumored to combine forces to spread bolita across the state."

"Illicit gambling. Isn't that within the purview of the FBI?"

The sheriff nodded affirmation.

"And yet, the notice comes from the state." Garland paused as he recalled and assimilated facts from years before. "I've got a friend in the FBI. She told me they were moving the management of the Jacksonville office to Miami. Her reason was that J. Edgar was angry you were too effective at law enforcement. Maybe. Just maybe, they are making room for Trafficante and his ilk to thrive in north Florida? All of the men involved in the Surrency murders were involved in bolita."

"Yeah, they draw numbers in Havana every day. We know the mob ties down there. I guess since the game is played offshore, there's a claim of no illegal activity taking place?"

Garland chuckled at a family memory. "My grandfather, A.D., gambled on what they called Havana in the panhandle.

Same as bolita." The prosecutor became pensive. "He had this book that assigned numbers to dreams. Whatever he dreamt about, the next morning he looked it up, found the number, and played it." He smiled. "I think it caused a sizeable rift between he and my grandmother."

"Demand is everywhere." When there was no response from Headley, the sheriff continued. "Do you think your prosecutor friend in Bartow has made any headway with the Swearingen case?"

Garland sighed. "I'm not sure how hard he's searching. Last time I was there he seemed pretty scared of the consequences of pursuing truth."

"And therein lies the rub. We as a society won't exist in honesty if we don't have warriors willing to sacrifice for truth. Integrity among densely populated areas seems to be cast aside in preference for immediacy. Lessons are learned on the farm. True prosperity takes time. Soil needs tilling. Attention to crops must be given for them to grow healthily."

The two men sat silently for several minutes. Each processed the task ahead.

Garland broke the silence. "What we need is a linchpin."

The sheriff picked up a single playing card that always sat on his desk. It was the ace of spades. He pinched it with his thumb and forefinger at the top, tapped the bottom on the surface of the desk, slid his fingers along its edge, flipped it over, and repeated the motion without end. Some believed the card possessed negative energy. The sheriff believed himself strong enough to deflect its strength onto his enemies, as was the case during his service in World War I. "Have you got any ideas what the keystone of our case might be?"

"No matter how much I think about it, I keep going back the Surrency's funeral. If we know why those men were there, maybe it'll break this wide open for us."

"When was the funeral?"

"November 29, 1936."

The sheriff thought momentarily. "We arrested all three of those boys on December 12, 1936. Maybe they needed to reiterate a threat to the family of not being exposed as greater conspirators? Maybe they needed to watch the Surrencys being lowered into the ground for confirmation?" He paused. "The possibilities are endless."

"Or they were telling Hysler they would financially back him throughout the appeals process for his continued silence?"

The sheriff nodded. "The possibilities are endless."

"Regardless, I think I'll have to go it alone from the legal perspective. I'm not sure if my friend is simply scared, or if he's been compromised and is trying to scare me off?"

27

Garland Headley walked from his desk to the windows against the far wall. Lifting one after another until all were open allowed the cool morning breeze to circulate in his office. It was April 8, 1941. Four years had passed since the conviction of Clyde Hysler for the murders of John and Mayme. Baker's conviction followed shortly after the man who hired him. The fate of death was ascribed to the least culpable coconspirator.

It was days like this the prosecutor enjoyed most. The reason people lived in Florida were the mild days during winter and spring. It was late enough in the cycle where temperatures would reach the mid-eighties. Garland knew he'd have to close the windows in the next hour or two. Choosing to sit on the sofa he spread paperwork on the coffee table between the two settees. Nothing compared to the verve of the Surrency trial. Life and career had sunk into mundaneness. Nhi offered his only respite. She was his ray of light.

Establishing truth in the affairs of society was the purpose of a career in law. Parents nor educators communicated with the prosecutor, the truly vile nature in which humans bastardized reality for personal benefit. It left him feeling ill-prepared when facing those who would do him, or God forbid Nhi, harm.

A slower case load offered the man time to reflect. Hindsight was 20/20, but the future was open to interpretation. He considered the souls of the five humans that converged as participants in the most horrific crime in the young city's history. Had death been final for the Surrencys? Logic spoke to the inequity of a greater good allowing evil to control the abrupt ending of human experience. Every fiber of Headley's being believed there was an eternal element to all humans.

Obsession over the Surrencys inspired the man to stand and walk to his desk. From the long, narrow center drawer he removed two photographs that had been given to him by John and Mayme's family. He lay them side-by-side on the desk's surface. Staring back at him were portraits of the couple. Both possessed contented smiles. Was there an invisible hand encouraging his actions after so many years?

Suddenly, a gust of wind blew through the open windows. It whipped around the four walls of the office until reaching the wall behind the man. Having nowhere else to go the gust blew across the desktop, disrupting the visages of his most famous charges. Garland lost sight of the photographs momentarily. Hurriedly, he scurried to the other side of his desk and searched the floor. Nothing but heart of pine planks stared back at him. Quickly he dropped to his knees and searched beneath the furniture. Nothing. He stood in the center of his office and pivoted three hundred and sixty degrees, casting his vision to the four corners of his office like a sweeping lighthouse beam. Nothing.

Frustrated, the man walked behind his desk and sat in his chair. Looking at its empty surface his eyes finally came to rest on the portrait of Nhi that brightened everything physical and ethereal about his life. Astonishingly, he saw the two photographs. John on the left, and Mayme on the right. Each tucked into the lower corners of the frame, as if placed there purposefully. Was there a message?

The attorney stood, took the framed photograph, and walked back to the sofa. He placed the picture that contained three visages gently on the coffee table, and then busied about retrieving the papers that had been scattered by the breeze.

Act of God was a legal term with which he was familiar. Garland was not concerned with the orderly retrieval of documents. Awareness of what his life had become was paramount. He tossed the stack of papers he'd collected in a haphazard manner atop the table's surface and hurriedly sat in front of the three photographs.

He stared at Nhi. The most beautiful and settled soul he'd ever known. In her visage was the antithesis of all he'd experienced during his career. John and Mayme represented the most troubling set of circumstances he was made to overcome.

Staring intently at the trinity before him, a connection between the three grew in his consciousness. As haphazard as the murders occurred, so was his meeting with the woman for which he felt immense love and respect. Nhi came into his life at a time when he needed her most. Law school training supported questioning all subjects until absolute truth emerged. Like an inverted pyramid, multiple possibilities were explored and cast aside until coming to a singular resolution. John and Mayme's energy brought the two humans together.

Garland wasn't sure Nhi needed him as much as he needed her. Had the murdered couple appreciated the manner in which he relentlessly pursued truth on their behalf? Nhi certainly had been a gift from a higher power. Was she sent to settle his burdened soul? Turmoil had been replete since experiencing the trials. Many times, Garland appreciated Nhi as having saved him from possibly spiraling into an irretrievable abyss.

Whenever destructive behavior was witnessed by Garland as an adolescent, his father would say, "people incapable of conceiving beauty, are consumed by destructive behavior. It is viewed by them as that which they create. Make sure you know how to appreciate the abundant beauty in the world." John and Mayme had been consumed by hatred beyond their control. Regardless of the genesis of Nhi and Garland's meeting, he would be forever grateful to the couple for exposing the manner in which the world truly operated.

Shaken from his appreciation of life's circumstances, he peered toward the other side of his office when he heard the door to his office opening. Through its void walked Sheriff Swift.

When the two men made eye contact, the prosecutor waved him over to the seating area in front of the open windows. The cop held a folder down by his side.

"What brings you to my end of Adams Street?" the prosecutor inquired.

"It's the gift that keeps on giving," the sheriff responded, sarcastically.

Garland's heart sank. "Which case is it?"

The sheriff responded with a smile. "The Surrency affair."

Incredulous, he asked, "what? That was over four years ago."

The sheriff dropped the folder on the coffee table in front of him as he sat down. "Apparently, Baker has recounted his story. He claims Hysler had nothing to do with the murder. It was simply motivated by opportunity."

Garland thought back to the evidence brought out at trial. "So, I guess he's saying they never knew Hysler?"

"Exactly."

"So, what about the dozen witnesses that saw Hysler together with Baker and Tyler that morning, before the murder occurred. What about the gas station manager that was arrested for perjury when he said he hadn't seen the three at the gas station that morning, when in fact, he had? How did they get the gun that had been in possession of the Hyslers?"

"Oh, it gets better than that." The sheriff smiled wryly. The situation seemed humorous to the man who knew truth to be on his side. "He's accusing me and my officers of beating them into confessing that Hysler was involved. He's accusing you of promising them they'd be off the chain-gang in three years' time, and the death penalty was off the table."

"The Florida Supreme Court upheld the conviction in February 1938, so they decide to change the circumstances of the case for the Supreme Court's review?" Garland questioned rhetorically. "If you would have told me in law school attorneys could be so corrupt, I would have laughed at you. Isn't it amazing what money can buy?"

"The Hysler's definitely have it." The sheriff shook his head. "I'm just not so sure it isn't being supplemented by some other source."

"Interesting. Tyler escapes, never to be heard from again. That pawn has been removed from the chess board, so he isn't available to contradict Baker's recanting of their story." The prosecutor nodded in frustration. "It's looking more and more like there was help from a much higher authority. Who was it that said, 'the whole world is a stage, and we are merely players?'"

The sheriff shook his head.

Garland broke the stare between the two and peered across his office toward his desk. What were the implications? Certainly, the Supreme Court would see beyond the ruse? Even if they did, there seemed to be an unlimited supply of money possessing the ability to create whatever fiction moved the case further up the appellate chain. At least there would be an end at the U.S. Supreme Court. Not until it was kicked back to them by the high court should they worry. Consternation was still present and borne of the manner in which the system can be manipulated by those with means.

"Did I ever tell you I grew up on a farm?" the prosecutor asked.

"Most of us did."

Garland nodded. "It was a different time then. What changed?"

"The federal reserve bank."

"What?"

"A centralized bank that flooded the country with money. Enacted in 1913. It took starry eyed youth from the farms, brought them into the cities where nothing is created but financialized securities and paperwork. The money emanating from that bank created the roaring twenties ... and the despair once money supply was contracted. People who didn't make the right trades jumped from windows of tall buildings having lost everything." The sheriff paused. "I think that was all done on purpose by those who control that bank to gauge people's reaction to the situation. There's no coincidence our country went to war shortly after the federal reserve was established. War is big business. Next thing you know they'll target the family farm. This environment in which we operate … the lies and deceptions built upon stacks of money, is the purview of evil."

The prosecutor asked rhetorically, "if we don't get control of it, what will happen to our children and grandchildren's future?"

The old man leaned back, allowing him to reach inside his coin pocket. From it he retrieved a 1933 United States one-ounce Gold Eagle coin. "When they outlawed and confiscated these things back in '33, I bought up and hoarded as many of these as I could. Owning something real, something tangible is the only thing that will save the American family from losing its wealth to paper dollars. I don't care what form of gold standard politicians say we're using; they will always print more money than the ratio allows."

"But that's illegal. We were told to turn in all of our gold when it became illegal to own."

The sheriff brushed aside his friend's condemnation in favor of his final comment. "I got into law enforcement because I thought it was a righteous pursuit. The older I get the more I realize farming is the most noble profession of all. Blood, sweat, and tears spent for the benefit of feeding humanity. It doesn't get any better than that."

Garland nodded his agreement slowly. Once again, the prosecutor spoke rhetorically. "I guess plowing the earth, embracing its fertility and creating growth beyond one's own existence is what life's all about."

28

December 8, 1941. Garland climbed the stairwell of his office building. In his right hand was his ubiquitous briefcase filled with various files of crimes yet to prosecute. The fifth anniversary of his successful prosecution of Clyde Hysler was just over two months away. The family put all of their resources into filing appeals from the appellate court, the Florida Supreme Court, and arguments were due in five days at the U.S. Supreme Court. Florida's attorney general would handle those proceedings, but Headley knew the outcome would affect his life; for better or worse.

Emerging the stairwell, the counselor made his way down the hall to the door of the office that contained his name. Entering he witnessed Holli Goldman's face as she peered intently at him from behind her desk. His assistant looked concerned.

"Good morning, Miss Goldman," he said as he walked past her desk, toward the door to his inner office.

"Morning, Sir. Your morning paper is on your desk." She paused, and under her breath she whispered, "God help us all."

Garland looked back at her curiously, as he closed the door between them. He walked over to his desk and placed his briefcase atop its surface. Squaring himself behind the desk, and aligning with the copy of the Times Union, he read the headline —JAPS BOMB PEARL HARBOR. He lifted it to reveal the copy of the Jacksonville Journal. The exact same caption stared up at him. It was wrong on so many levels. The prosecutor reached over and activated the intercom on his desk. "Holli." He was never so informal at the office. "Can you please get Nhi on the phone."

"Yes sir," came the reply.

Casting all decorum aside, and forgoing the use of the intercom, Garland's assistant came into his office to tell him that Nhi was waiting for him on the phone.

The boss picked up the receiver while motioning for Holli to have a seat. War was imminent. It was human nature to want those you cared about close.

Holli witnessed only her boss' side of the conversation. She heard him ask, "Is your family okay?" He listened. "I know they must be upset." Listening. "Do you think it would be alright for me to come to your house tonight." Listening, he smiled curtly at Holli. "I understand," he completed before hanging up the telephone.

"Is she okay?" his assistant inquired.

He nodded. "As well as can be expected, I guess."

He sat in his oversized executive chair and stared at his assistant. Never at a loss for words, or an assessment of any situation he faced, Garland Headley didn't know what to say other than, "so much for George Washington's no foreign entanglements plea."

Ever the realist, Holli offered a chilling assessment. "It's almost like they knew this was coming. Why else would they have begun conscripting young men last year. They were building a ready fighting force."

Garland nodded agreement. He stared across the room at the fireplace, and two sofas, where so many strategy sessions occurred. "Holli, I'm beginning to believe there is an invisible hand moving chess pieces across the globe. I've spent my career, albeit a young one, feeling like I can make a difference by prosecuting people like Clyde Hysler. As I gain more and more experience it seems obvious to me the people we deal with are like ants in an anthill. Someone above is holding a magnifying glass, ready to fry anyone for the purpose of not exposing the greater conspiracy."

"That's pretty grim, Garland."

He shook his head. "Not if the world's population becomes aware."

"How would that happen?"

He shook his head. "I don't know. The only way of communicating globally," he picked up the paper from his desk, "is this." He looked directly into the eyes of his assistant. "Did you ever go see Citizen Kane, back in September?"

"Yeah. Great film."

Garland nodded. "It speaks volumes to the fact one man has so much control over what we read and understand about the world."

"I hadn't thought about that." Attempting to shift the conversation, she inquired, "are you going to see Nhi tonight?"

"Nhi." His girlfriend flashed into his consciousness. "Man, what she and her family must be going through."

"Are they okay?"

"She wouldn't say. You know, Japanese stoicism."

The two sat silently for several moments before Garland pierced the silence. "The Supreme Court is supposed to hear the Hysler case in four days. I wonder if that will get delayed?"

"I hope not," Holli exclaimed.

Garland looked curiously at her, wondering from where her emotion emanated. "Why so interested in the case?"

The assistant shook her head, feeling almost guilty. "It's just that I've seen how that case affected you over the last five years."

"Hmmm. Thank you." He paused. "I think I've let it get the better of me because I feel like the Surrency family deserves better." He shook his head. "Noble Enge is dead because of it … because of me. This world just isn't what it seems, Holli."

The young assistant drew in and exhaled a deep breath. "We can only do our best."

The two sat silently, contemplating the meaning of the world and how they fit within it. Garland's thoughts drifted to Nhi, and then to the day they met. Memories sparked pleasantly until he recalled one item from that day. He reached over to his righthand desk drawer and pulled it open. He leaned over and began to rummage through its contents. Years of accumulated items lay atop that which he sought. Pushing aside smaller items and removing larger ones, he finally cleared a bare space at the bottom.

There was no smile at the site of the item that lay dormant for years. From his open drawer he retrieved the cigarette card with Hitler's visage. Guilt over littering his town caused him to retrieve it the day he'd tossed it onto the sidewalk. He examined it for nearly a minute before handing it across the desk to his assistant.

"A friend of mine gave me a pack of German cigarettes several years ago. I decided to open it and try one the day I met Nhi. This card was inside the pack." He laughed. "I guess simply possessing that card now would place me under suspicion of the FBI?"

"You're joking, right?"

He became pensive, and slowly shook his head. "I wish I were." Garland looked Holli squarely in the eyes. "It's very scary that a national organization can operate above reproach. They become whatever law suits their agenda." Then he admitted, "life was simpler on the farm."

Miss Goldman laid the card on her boss' side of the desk. "You're not thinking of going back, are you?"

Garland's gaze drifted again to the fireplace setting. All of the meetings held there flooded his consciousness. There was so much good he wished to do. He considered Holli's question in the context of life goals when compared to that which it had become. Two grifters who committed murder had a greater understanding of how the world worked. For all of his education, never once did he understand evil wanted control, total control. "I honestly don't know, Holli."

29

Early in the evening of the eighth of December Garland made his way quickly from the office to the Kurosawa's home. The prosecutor was at odds with life and career. It was time for him to take a stand and unify with those he considered family. The United States was now at war with Japan. Lines would be drawn by the overarching authority of the federal government. Having watched the FBI's failed attempt to exert its influence in Jacksonville offered the man's critical mind fuel to question motives.

As a youngster he never understood how the assassination of Archduke Ferdinand caused the world to plunge into the War to End All Wars. He was completely unknown to ninety-nine percent of the population, yet his death dictated global war. Calls to unify against a common enemy fell flat on Garland. He'd met and courted the one woman who opened pathways to something greater than the two of them. It had been over three years since their formal introduction. Both of Garland's parents were dead, and he had no siblings. Nothing in his life spoke to family. It rendered the man incapable of visualizing a family of his own, until that day. He wasn't about to sacrifice their relationship to a government he'd grown to understand was corrupt to its core.

Nhi taught the man to raise the level of his mind to that of the universe. Perspective dictated he envision the pain on both sides of any conflict. As he drove closer to the Saint Johns River, and the Kurosawa home, he considered all of the American families who would lose sons, brothers, and uncles. His assessment was not limited to that which was familiar. Japanese families would feel the same pain.

Worldly focus shifted to Hitler and his German army. There would be multiple fronts on which to fight. Jacksonville's population neared two hundred thousand. Citizens to which he felt responsible. How many multiples of his city would be lost fighting the second great war? Determination to protect the woman he loved pushed all other considerations from his mind.

Garland maneuvered his car left down Osceola Street, and eventually onto River Drive. It was a path he'd become familiar over the course of his three-year courtship of Nhi. As the vehicle came to a stop in front of the dock that extended into the river, he placed the transmission in first gear, turned the wheels to the curb, and set the brake. Looking through the passenger's side window, he saw Mr. Kurosawa at the pier's end. Emerging, he closed the driver's door and moved around its front to make his way toward the man he respected and hoped would one day be family.

Garland saw Niko leaning against the railing, staring at his boat undulating violently in the tumultuous river. "Mr. Kurosawa," he called.

The old man didn't move.

Slowly, Garland moved next to his friend and took up a similar position. He said nothing, deferring to the patriarch. If the man felt compelled to speak, he would.

Several minutes of silence passed before the man conceived English words to communicate to his daughter's courter. "This boat represents my most American possession." He translated the next sentence in his mind. "I admit, I came to Jacksonville because I saw an opportunity to profit. I've grown to love my adopted city."

"I can protect your family. I'm the state's attorney for God's sake."

The old man smiled, still staring at the craft below. "I appreciate your devotion to my daughter, but that is not how the world works. I left Japan due to the oppressive nature of our government. I came to the land of opportunity."

Garland sensed there was a lot more to be said and allowed Niko all the time he needed to communicate his feelings.

He pointed to the boat below. "I drove this boat every day to our factory in Green Cove Springs. We employ thirty-seven Americans. Thirty-seven American families can create the life they've envisioned for themselves because of the hard work of all of us." Niko finally broke his stare upon the vessel and shifted to Garland. "This morning I pick up the newspaper and feel like an enemy of the state."

"Mr. Kurosawa, I'm sure the government, the FBI knows you're a loyal American citizen." No sooner did the words leave his mouth did he understand the hypocrisy contained therein.

"Do you know, Garland, what we make at our plant?"

"You make carburetors."

"Yes. We make carburetors for the Japanese Military."

Garland drew in and exhaled a deep breath. He then dropped his head into his right hand and massaged his forehead. "That makes things a little more difficult."

In an angry tone, Mr. Kurosawa uttered something in his native tongue.

Garland surmised it was something to the effect of, "no shit, dumbass."

Niko settled down and returned his gaze to the Chris Craft below. He pointed to the boat. "Do you know the freedom this represents? The only boundary is the water. Nhi always enjoyed driving it on the river every weekend. I guess those days are over."

"As dire as the situation seems now, and even with the corruption inherent in government, I don't see the citizens allowing them to jail you."

"Oh, my dear prosecutor friend, I think you will be stunned how easily a population will coalesce against those seen as a threat. Many atrocities will be revealed in the decades to come. It's part of the global chessboard. We are merely pawns moved at whim to advance elite goals." He paused. "I have many contacts in the Japanese military … in their intelligence apparatus. They tell me the plans have already been drawn up to imprison Japanese Americans for the duration of the war. All they must do is convince FDR it is the right move. As an industrialist supplying the enemy's military, they will come for me first."

"I'm not about to stop fighting."

"And they count on that. You will be branded subversive and eliminated to the cheers of all who embrace the corrupt government."

"What can we do?"

"We? I will take care of my family. You move on with your American life."

"No."

The old man from an ancient culture glanced sharply at his young visitor. Contradiction was never tolerated.

"I love your daughter, and I will fight to make sure nothing happens to her."

The old man softened his tone. "Maybe you are the only one who can ensure her safety."

"Is it okay if I go inside and speak with her?"

Niko nodded his head. His stare drifted back toward the boat. The blank look that'd occupied his countenance for hours returned and isolated the old man.

Garland hesitated briefly. He'd become accustomed to Japanese tradition and wondered if a bow was called for in this situation. Shaking away indecision, he moved back down the long pier. Adjusting his route around the front of his car, he crossed the street after looking both ways. The long sidewalk that led to the house couldn't be traversed quickly enough. Concern for Nhi occupied is thoughts throughout the day.

Although he cared for the Kurosawas as a family, her energy was what set his soul on the path to freedom.

Stopping at the front door, he removed his shoes by placing each foot on the opposite heel and prying them off one-by-one. Quickly he removed his socks and dropped them onto the shoes. Garland reached for the lion-head door knocker and tapped exactly three times. He saw shadows through the ornate cut glass moving toward the entry.

The door opened to reveal Mrs. Kurosawa. Greetings were exchanged and the woman allowed Garland entry. He walked down the hallway and found Nhi in the parlor sitting alone on the sofa. The couple were not allowed to be together in the room with the door closed. Garland moved toward the woman he loved and sat next to her.

"I spoke to your father."

"What did he say?"

"He told me I needed to leave and allow him to take care of the family."

Nhi's heart sank. "Are you leaving?"

"Never."

She smiled genuinely, and her eyes glistened and radiated warmth. "What are we going to do?"

"Nothing … not until we know what the government's stance is."

"What does father say? I saw you two talking on the dock."

Garland drew in and exhaled a deep breath. The thought of possibly losing Nhi to an encampment was almost too much to bear. Regardless he knew he would never stop loving her. "He seems to believe all the Japanese Americans will be rounded up and imprisoned in camps."

Nhi uttered something in Japanese Garland assumed was a plea to a greater deity.

"Nhi?"

"Yes."

"Do you trust me completely?"

She thought briefly. "Yes, implicitly."

"How long have we known each other?"

"Over three years."

"Is that long enough for me to ask your father for your hand in marriage?"

The woman blushed. "Are you sure?"

"From the first day I saw you outside the jail in downtown Jacksonville. That certainty has only grown over our time together."

"Why now?"

"Out of respect for your father. Your family will become my family, and then he may allow me to help."

"What can you do to help?"

He held up his hand gently pushing back at her inquiry. "There are a lot of moving pieces to my plan, but once I'm sure I can make it happen I will bring it to the family."

"But you will need to be a part of the family."

"Yes." Garland stood and walked toward the open door to the parlor.

Nhi called to him. "When will you ask my father?"

"Now," he called back.

Nhi hurried excitedly to the front windows of the home. One might call it instinct; others would accuse the older women of eavesdropping. Nhi's two elders joined her at the window and watched Garland make his way down the sidewalk, across the street, and to the dock's end. When they saw the two men speaking cordially, all three women looked at one another and smiled. Genuine happiness filled the home at a time when desperation could have destroyed the family.

30

Rumblings concerning the preparation of internment camps grew louder within the legal community. Garland was certain the Kurosawas would be taken west, how far he did not know. Even if they were taken to Arkansas, it would destroy their family and the business they'd built. Varied conceptions of the circumstances Japanese Americans would be forced to endure caused a great deal of stress for the prosecutor. He knew if discussions were happening in Washington, the plan to imprison Americans was a forgone conclusion. It would be mere weeks before the roundup began. Worst case, apprehending Japanese Americans would resemble that of the Bolsheviks gathering and exterminating political rivals.

Love between Garland and Nhi was pure. She'd been brought up in a culture whereby men controlled the family. In Garland's estimation, subservience did not lead to strength. It was not for him to argue with the ancient culture his soon-to-be father-in-law embraced. His wife, however, would experience more freedom within their home. Denying the woman who'd instilled a sense of wonder upon their first meeting possessed a great deal of value within the universe. If God was to bless the couple with children, her positive influence would be paramount in their development.

Garland's love for his fiancé drove his desire to ensure she had a traditional Japanese wedding. If he could not provide that for her, he wouldn't be the husband she'd dreamed of since childhood. Preparations were made by the three women. Joy permeated the household and Garland worried his warnings had fallen on deaf ears.

The United States Supreme Court controlled the conviction of Clyde Hysler and its resulting death penalty. It would be the final chapter in the saga of John and Mayme Surrency. He'd always held himself out as a champion of due process. Beliefs that all humans should have equal opportunity for justice permeated the man's soul. Bastardization of the legal process did nothing to damage the man's resolve. It only brought to light the corrupt nature of governments, and the danger in trusting politicians. Nineteenth century British politician Lord Acton summarized what many had written before. Power corrupts; absolute power corrupts absolutely. It was a saying his parents instilled in him as a young boy. Not until he'd experienced the power of corruption, and how it damaged his career, did the true meaning become clear.

A Shinto temple had been constructed at the far end of the Kurosawa's backyard. All preparations had been meticulously made. Guests were few. Only those who were trusted were invited. Sheriff Swift sat in the second row on the groom's side. Margaret Slater sat to his right. Holli Goldman was there. The wedding hadn't even begun, and she employed the use of a tissue. Miriam Enge brought Ted, Bess, Carol, and Kathy.

Few local Japanese friends sat behind the bride's family. Trusted workers from the Green Cove Springs factory attended the wedding.

The bride wore a white wedding kimono, and the groom deferred to tradition, donning a black ceremonial kimono. Hiding Nhi's face from all except the groom was a wataboshi. An egg-shaped hood completely covered her face as she walked down the aisle. Once she joined Garland, she lifted her head. His vision of her tingled within his soul. Conception of her beauty had not waned since the day he first beheld the countenance of a woman whose soul emanated strength.

The ceremony was presented in both Japanese and English. No one minded doubling the length of the ceremony. Even Holli wasn't all cried out by the time the wedding ended.

Afterward, guests milled about the backyard enjoying the Kurosawa's hospitality. Laughter and joy were embraced among those who'd been made to endure a nearly six year long ordeal.

Garland couldn't help but stare at his wife. Her beauty conveyed an eternal quality. Something within her expressed generations past, and a future without conclusion. Just as the memory of John and Mayme would occupy his soul eternally, he knew that he and Nhi would be inextricably linked forever. A couple who he never met played such an important role in his life. He thought once more of the wind blowing their photographs onto the picture of Nhi on his desk. It was a sign. Garland smiled, reached into an inner pocket in his kimono and retrieved those same photographs. He smiled at the countenances staring up at him. They seemed to return the gesture.

Happiness was interrupted when a servant emerged from the house. She walked over to Niko and whispered something to him. Keenly aware of all happenings, Garland watched his father-in-law intently. The two men made eye-contact. The patriarch bowed and dismissed the servant. He walked over to the prosecutor. "Army personnel from Camp Blanding are here."

"It's time."

"Are you sure your plan will work?"

Garland shook his head. "No, but it's our only hope." He looked to the fifteen-year-old Ted and motioned for the young boy to come to him. When the boy stood next to him, Garland asked. "Are you up for the task?"

Without a word, the boy nodded.

"What is it you're not supposed to forget?"

"The ammo box stashed in the boathouse storage locker."

"Remember, it's about forty pounds. Can you handle it?

"I may not look it, but I'm strong."

Ted ran double time around the side of the house, dragging along his polio riddled left leg. The bridegroom assembled his new family. Three women and two men didn't bother bidding adieu to their guests. They hurried past the make-shift Shinto temple and into the alleyway that ran behind the homes. Parked there was Garland's 1938 Plymouth.

Slowly, methodically, the son-in-law drove his new family down to Osceola Street, turned right and then left onto Riverside Drive. He envisioned army personnel searching the house. Questions proliferated in his mind. Were they destroying the home? Had they stationed a soldier at the dock? Was Ted able to get to the boat?

Garland constantly checked his rear and side view mirrors for signs of anyone chasing them. Without drawing attention to the vehicle, he slowly traversed the winding roads of the city. The river's undulating influence affected all that was built along its shores. A smile grew on his face when he saw the Saint Johns River Bridge come into sight. Once over the expanse, they were closer to completing the first stage of the plan. The only question was who would be waiting to greet them?

Nervous glances between driver and passengers were constant. Resolution that escaping was better than that which awaited the family in internment camps.

Garland turned left onto Chaseville Road and travelled nearly one mile to Merrill Road. Another left and he propelled the car toward the river. At its end, the road yielded to a stately home situated on the river. He entered and drove to the end of the driveway. The home's owner, Susanna James, was standing at the end of the dock with Axle Enge, the brother of murdered Noble.

The wedding party emerged from the car and walked across the lawn and to the end of the dock.

"Any sign of Ted?"

Axle just shook his head.

Garland smiled at the homeowner. "Thank you for allowing us to use your property, Mrs. James."

"It's my pleasure, Mr. state's attorney."

The woman's words stung. Since the bombing of Pearl Harbor, Garland had been focused on saving his wife and her family. He was forced to consider the fact his career was over. All that he'd worked so hard to build was gone.

"Here he comes," Axle broke the silence.

Everyone looked across the river. The Kurosawa's low profile Chris Craft could be barely seen in the distance. As it moved closer, Garland looked beyond it for vessels in pursuit. There appeared to be none.

The boy expertly guided the boat next to the dock and the questions began.

His uncle asked, "Is there anyone following you?"

The boy nodded. "Yeah." He looked at everyone in the crowd, maturely addressing each member of the party. "I took them down Jackson's creek."

"But it's too shallow," Axle implored.

The boy smiled. "They're in a big, deep draft boat. I think I got 'em grounded, but I have no idea how long it will take them to free themselves."

Garland asked, "were there any soldiers on the dock?"

"Just one."

"How'd you get past him?"

Ted smiled. "I pushed him in the river."

Garland chuckled. The wedding party quickly entered the boat young Ted vacated moments earlier. Axle called down to them. "My buddy has a fifty-foot boat that will get you where you're going. Remember, around the bend at Reddie Point he'll be waiting. That'll offer the opportunity to change boats without being seen by pursuers. Just don't dilly-dally."

Niko felt compelled to stand in the boat and bow to the man.

"Thank you for all your help," Garland called as the boat drifted away from the dock.

"Thank you for your tireless pursuit of justice," Axle replied.

Ted called to the bridegroom, "the ammo box you wanted is under the console."

Axle, Ted, and Mrs. James stood on the dock and watched the boat disappear into the distance. Irony was not lost on the man whose family was from Norway. He'd helped a family from Japan escape a government that deemed them enemies. Only a fellow immigrant truly understood the passion one held for an adopted homeland. The consideration of patriotism among migrants had been summarily dismissed by an institution who desired nothing, except control.

31

It was nearly a month after the wedding and the disappearance of the man who'd grown to be Sheriff Swift's friend. Upon his return to his office the day after the wedding he ordered a large, paper, world map to be hung on his wall. A pin with a red bead at its end marked the city of Jacksonville. Its purpose was to spark the sheriff's imagination to all possible places his friend might travel with his new bride and her family. A pin with a yellow bead marked Tokyo, Japan. He knew it unlikely Mr. Kurosawa would return to a homeland he felt betrayed him. Would Garland set up shop as a lawyer wherever he ended up settling? The world was the oyster of the young couple. Spirit moved humans to discovery. Genuine hope that his friends found freedom from dogmatic society brought a smile to the face of the grizzled law enforcement officer every time he looked at the map. A small modicum of jealousy permeated the man's soul.

Deputies passed through his office throughout the day. Updating the sheriff on petty crimes was the monotony that had become his career. Fantasies centered around Garland and Nhi were especially intense. The Supreme Court was due to issue their ruling on Hysler's appeal. He'd read the arguments put forth to the court on December 12, 1941; five short days after the Japanese bombed Pearl Harbor. It was an event that set in motion the escape of a man he'd appreciated for embracing all that was just for the people of Jacksonville.

The new state's attorney was just as young as Garland when he assumed the lofty role in the community. The sheriff approached eight years in his position. Enough time passed to give the man the opportunity to surround himself with those he trusted. Skepticism abounded in a man who'd come to understand federal law enforcement was not there to help local authorities. It was meant to centralize control of states that had been guaranteed independence in the Constitution. Just how far removed were those possessing the hidden hand of hegemony?

Swift stood from his desk and made his way around to the map on the wall. He placed his finger next to the red pin. The size of the boat on which they escaped had enough fuel to reach south Florida. He slid his fingertip across the paper, bouncing it along the east coast of Florida at potential stops. Palm Coast, Daytona, Vero Beach, Titusville, Melbourne, Palm Bay, West Palm and down to Miami. Each coastal city had adequate facilities for refueling. He knew there was no way they would travel north along the coast or attempt to cross the Atlantic.

From Miami, the man's finger drew an imaginary line to Havana, Cuba. He gauged the expanse between the island nation and South America. Could the boat travel the distance without refueling? He had no idea. Refueling in Jamaica was an option.

No matter what global city entered his consciousness, Rex Swift could easily imagine his friends thriving and happy wherever they alighted from the boat.

Local bulletins had been posted for the Kurosawa family. The sheriff knew no police forces in faraway lands would bother hunting down ersatz fugitives from intolerant tyranny. There seemed to be freedom beyond the borders of the United States the sheriff never imagined as a young soldier placing his life on the line. The country was in a second world war. His military service was meant to ensure war would no longer be an option. Marketing slogans brought the country together in its determination to stop evil. If war was never meant to cease, from where did malevolence gain control of the world? What conflicts would the children and grandchildren of the future face?

Sheriff Swift was shaken back into reality when the intercom burst to life with the voice of Holli Goldman. She'd moved over to his office after the new state's attorney was appointed. He wanted to bring in his own personnel. People he trusted to apply the law as he saw fit. "Margaret Slater is here to see you, sheriff."

Rex walked to his desk, flipped the switch on the intercom, and replied, "send her in."

The door to the office opened, and in walked a woman the sheriff only met a few times. She held a bundle of about fifty pages of paper in her hand. "The Supreme Court ruling came over the telex. I thought I'd bring you a copy."

The man took the stack of papers, moved behind his desk, and sat down. Studiously, he scanned the pages for the result. It read like the maintenance manual of his fleet of Plymouth patrol cars. Frustrated, he threw up his hands. "What does this all mean?"

"It means you get to execute those two bastards as soon as the state schedules it."

A smile grew on the man's face, until he realized there should be three people put to death for the murders of John and Mayme Surrency. "Tyler should be dead too."

"Yeah. Ironic. The one who pulled the trigger … seven times. He had murder in his heart the entire time. I guess we'll never know the true reason why?"

Sheriff Swift spoke to the air around him, and not directly to his visitor. "Yeah, if I could just get my hands on him. I'd find out why."

As the sheriff continued to scan the pages of the Supreme Court opinion, the name Alvin Tyler jumped from its surface in one particular place. It was that which grated his nerves. "Tyler broke jail and has apparently remained a fugitive from justice," it read.

Rex looked up at Margaret. "You were good friends with Garland. You wouldn't happen to know where they ended up settling?"

Margaret shook her head. "No. Why?"

"I'd just like to let him know we got two of the three."

She nodded. "He would like to know. Maybe we'll get to tell him one day."

32

As was customary in 1942 Florida juris prudence, the sheriff of the county in which capital crimes were committed was given the honor of throwing the switch that sent over two thousand volts of electricity through the bodies of criminals presumed irredeemable. Sheriff Swift stood in the fifteen-by-fifteen-foot room along with the warden and the prison's priest.

It was June 15, 1942, just over three months after the United States Supreme Court upheld the conviction and death penalty of Clyde Hysler.

The walls were concrete block painted yellow. The wall which the chair faced contained a large picture window. Families of victims were afforded the opportunity to witness the final gasps of men who'd taken life from innocent humans. Curtains were drawn closed until the time the prisoner was strapped into the device.

Few words were spoken between the men. An analogue clock on the wall marked the time until execution. The warden stood next to a table with a black telephone. Its only connection was to the governor's office. The Hysler family feared Governor Spessard Holland was too preoccupied with war efforts to give their son's case proper attention. The family used a significant amount of their ill-gotten gains to ensure their son's freedom. They'd finally resigned themselves to the fact he'd be made to pay for his crimes; and be the patsy sacrificed for the survival of the much larger criminal organization.

The door to the chamber opened and two burley guards led the young man inside. His normally florid face was flushed. Sweat beaded and dripped from his forehead. Fear emanated from his eyes as he looked at the three men in attendance. Sheriff Swift's only compassion was borne in the realization the young man's brain only recently fully formed. There was a higher power manipulating young people into deeds only meant to benefit elite. All should be made to pay.

The priest said a prayer of absolution as the guards strapped the young man into the chair. Whimpers could be heard from beneath the leather hood that covered his face. The only strength the young boy had shown during life was threats based in illegal activities. He knew he had the backing of a crime family filled with men who'd committed murder and been murdered. Violence was resolution. Although he'd not held the proverbial sword during the Surrencys' murder, he was the catalyst for the act. Blame was meant to befall two Black men. Lesser humans in the boy's estimation. Empathy rang hollow within the soul of a man who profited feeding the addictions of humans in need of help. He existed on the evil end of the energy spectrum, and its consuming flame would release his soul to a fate which only God determined.

Curtains separating the death chamber with the outer observation room were drawn open one minute before the appointed execution time. In the audience were Hysler family members. His mother wept openly. His father sat stoically, displaying the same florid face he'd passed down to his son. Winder Surrency, the brother of the murdered man, and well-known Sarasota attorney sat watching the proceedings. Many empty chairs were scattered about the gallery. Swift knew that one of them should be occupied by Garland Headley. He hoped his friend would get word that two men died that day.

A mere thirty minutes after the execution of Clyde Hysler, his coconspirator, James Baker was brought in to die in the same chair that released the soul of the man who'd hired him and his friend to commit robbery. Ironically, the only person who'd expressed hesitation to the crime, attempted to stop Tyler from moving forward with the plan, and expressed remorse to the family, would be put to death on the same day. Only the man who'd expressed violence in a lethal manner was able to live his life freely.

Sheriff Swift completed his constitutional duties on that day. His conscience was clear. He knew the men to be guilty. John Surrency emerged from his car with benevolence in his heart. A man who wished to help stranded souls was murdered by deeply flawed humans.

33

1950, Pinar del Rio, Cuba. The city was situated forty miles southwest of Havana. Stories of the mafia graft and corruption consumed the capital city and made natives skeptical of Americans. Garland proved himself as a valuable member of the community through hard work and his devotion to his Asian family. The family farm consisted of seventy-five hectares of land planted in tobacco. Escaping Jacksonville with nothing more than the clothes on their backs, the extended family had one valuable possession secured by Ted Enge during their escape. It was the metal ammo box filled with 1933 one-ounce gold eagle coins.

Occasionally, Garland considered the use of the precious metal to purchase the farm. Memories of his friend Rex Swift always carrying a coin in his pocket for luck brought a smile to his face. It was the only time he'd been dishonest with his friend. Possessing an item deemed illegal by the government wasn't such an awful breach when considering the law's purpose was to weaken the fortunes of hard-working families. Something spoke to the adult about possessing that which was real. As a child he'd toiled in the dirt on his family farm. Earth caked beneath his fingernails offered a constant reminder of the reward for hard work. It wasn't difficult for the young man to recognize the relationship between utilizing the earth to bring forth prosperity. That which the planet possessed offered generational wealth to all who appreciated it. Success was not a flash in the pan. It was a long-term proposition secured across generations.

Cuban farmers did not see others as competition, but resources upon which to draw. It was the sense of community the family appreciated most. Upon harvest dried tobacco leaves were taken to market and sold to the finest cigar manufacturers in the world.

Garland and Nhi welcomed a son, Niko, and daughter, Kimiko. The children were six and three, respectively.

Years were spent preparing the farm for cultivation. The rich soil beneath surface growth provided a fertile environment that replenished nutrient rich crops seasonally. The blank slate upon which the family's vision was built offered the opportunity to construct houses as unique as the family. Garland and Nhi's dwelling combined colonial and Asian influences while the grandparent's home was traditional Japanese. Between the two was a traditional Shinto temple for prayer and meditation.

Spanish was learned by all members of the family. For the second time the Kurosawas embraced an adopted homeland. As the family grew, subsequent generations benefitted from global exposure. The children were fluent in three languages. Worldly views instilled at a young age provided the children opportunity for success no matter which part of the globe they settled.

Nhi road bikes with the children into town every morning. Little Niko enjoyed school with Cuban classmates. From the age of six months, Kimiko occupied a baby seat on the back of her mother's bike. At three, she insisted on her own mode of transportation. Nhi tethered a rope between the two in order to pull her at a speed adequate for on time arrival.

Saturdays the family drove into Havana to shop at the farmer's market. The kids insisted on a treat each week. Mostly they enjoyed mojito shortbread bars. Powdered sugar dusted on top of the dessert stuck to the noses and upper lips and provided great joy to the brother and sister as they laughed at one another.

Farming brought Garland back to his roots. It grounded him in all that was right about God. Bringing together the influences of the universe to grow for the benefit of humanity provided the most benevolent self-expression.

Colorful tented canopies aligned the aisles of the farmer's market. Cubans of all shades strolled systematically viewing the vegetables of each vendor, assessing personal needs for the next week. Little Niko sat atop Garland's shoulders. Headstrong Kimiko strolled independently next to her mother, never straying too far. Every hundred yards or so the girl asked to be held until her legs rested enough to express her individuality once again.

Garland would not change a single moment of his life. Choices were questioned, but he had the most beautiful and loving family for which he could hope. Energy surrounded him no longer contained destructive shades associated with career criminals. Throughout their days together Garland found himself staring at Nhi. Her countenance was flawless, and he finally understood it to reflect her energy within, emanating the happiness she embraced. He wished he could be so content, but his soul had been tainted beyond repair. Had their souls been eternally intertwined? When his energy was finally released upon death, would it be cleansed of experiences tainted by flawed human flesh?

Long walks down one aisle mirrored trips through adjacent lanes. Seemingly aimless progress was interrupted by focus when items of need were spied. Children were handed between parents as they took turns negotiating purchases. Each adult wore a backpack. They were slowly filled as shopping brought forth bounty.

The final turn was into the corridor of a dilapidated, corrugated tin building. It was the only structure that signaled permanence and was used as the keystone upon which the rest of the market was constructed weekly. Individual stalls lined each side of the building bifurcated by the aisle through which the family strolled. Vendors offered more durable goods in this building. Inventory could be locked and stored indefinitely. Tools and other implements were available for any task around the many farms that dotted the countryside. Even rifles for hunting could be purchased within the building.

Bright Caribbean sunshine burst through the door at the far end of the building and grew in intensity as the family completed their shopping for the week. Glare obstructed Garland's view, but his heart began to race as he conceived a sight he'd never considered in Cuba.

The only stain on the Island nation was the massive corruption contained in Havana. Brought forth by the American Mafia, the former prosecutor knew of its existence. It was his job to teach his children of its evil intent, and they should never associate with such men. No matter how romantic the lure of easy money and good times, physical attachments faded with aging visages. All that was based in pleasure was meant to dissipate without permanence. That which lasts forever is associated with the energy released from human bondage upon death. Garland looked at his stunning wife and offered a muted smile. It was his hope their children possessed the sensibility of a culture many thousands of years older than his.

Twenty paces in front of the family were three men he thought he'd never see together. Santo Trafficante fled to the safety of Cuban casinos when the heat became too great in Florida. Walking next to the mobster was a young Havana attorney named Fidel Castro. Garland knew the reputation of the man he'd read about in local papers. He seemed to be saying all the right things about the need to secure the future of Cuba for Cubans. The fact the two of them were together initiated the question of, "why?" It was the third man who stood at a booth lifting and assessing the quality of rifles that shuttered the man's soul. In the trial for the murders of John and Mayme Surrency, one witness referred to this man's skin color as that of ginger cake. The description was spot on, and Garland Headley found himself staring at a free Alvin Tyler. A man known to be a thug for hire and speculated to be working directly with the FBI.

The former prosecutor smiled at the realization Grady Judd's assertion was presented for him to behold. Truth will always find the light of day.

Garland glanced at the fresh and innocent faces of his children. For all he'd done to protect them, and provide a future of freedom, there was an indication dictatorship was being imported to the island nation. Was Tyler there to assassinate anyone who stood in the way of those wishing to take control?

Patriarch Niko insisted on teaching martial arts to his grandchildren. It was the only bone of contention between him and his son-in-law. Suddenly, Garland was happy his children were on a path to becoming strong and self-reliant. His epiphany was one that carried forth for generations. No matter the zeitgeist, evil always advanced its influence upon those accepting it. The only way to counteract malevolently drawing humanity into pleasures of the flesh, was to teach their children value comes from within. Happiness is based in energy. Physical pleasure is fleeting. Existing as a mere human will destroy a soul's destiny upon death, and evil will be ever-present to exploit weakness.

John and Mayme Surrency instilled a greater passion for justice in Garland Headley. More importantly, they offered a glimpse into eternity. The couple offered a bridge upon which his life travelled. Beset on his life's journey were all manner of criminal. Witnessing Alvin Tyler brandishing a weapon was disheartening, yet the scene strengthened his courage. Clearer came the resolution he must always fight to protect his family from the evil wishing to knock the Godly from righteousness.

The man who'd run from corruption, understood it would always be a part of life. He'd emerged from the family farm as an idealistic young lawyer. Retrospect offered memories of times he'd been approached to perform questionable legal actions. Refusal placed a target on his back. The fact he was incorruptible limited the furtherance of his career into loftier political positions. Printed money flowed into the campaigns of those who had no qualms of selling the influence their position offered.

For eight years living in Cuba, the man felt safe existing in his adopted homeland. Not once did he feel he'd ever again be called to action. Steadfast became his understanding he'd likely be made to fight, and this time confrontation may prove violent. Garland resolved to protect his family physically, just as John Surrency had done.

He looked admiringly again at Nhi, Niko, and Kimiko. Comfortable was the man certain, no matter what his earthly fate held, the four of them would know one another eternally.

Postscript

I first heard the story of John and Mayme Surrency on the occasion of my first date with a woman who was their great-granddaughter. Superficial details were shared over dinner. Although a tragic occurrence, my interest that night was the beautiful woman sitting across from me. Flash forward twenty-three years and we have been together ever since; twenty-two years as husband and wife.

Having reached a point in life whereby I've moved toward my passion for writing, my wife suggested I take a look at the Surrency Affair. On its surface, the story seemed to be intriguing and worthy of prose. When I began to research the events surrounding the murder of John and Mayme, there were a lot of circumstances that caused consternation.

The names of those involved in the murder, both victim and perpetrators, as well as the family members are actual names. Through marriage, several of the extended family members who were children at the time, are (and were) people I call(ed) family and deserve recognition and respect. I've changed the names of those beyond the scope of the family tragedy as the frontline to where fiction begins.

We've all read books and watched movies whereby we've questioned, "did that really happen?" Some of what you've read in this novella might seem extraordinary, and impossible to fathom. Readers may feel facts put forth in this story are outlandish. Truth is sometimes stranger than fiction, and it can write itself with little added examination. When researching this novel and digesting facts as reported in the media of the day, questions became worthy of consideration, and all are validly acknowledged.

The first question centered on the fact that John and Mayme were murdered the day before Thanksgiving, 1936. Possessing a benevolent heart, it struck me odd even the most hardened criminal would set out to rob and murder someone the day before an occasion centered around family. As with victims whose demise were the result of over-kill; the circumstances around this murder appeared all too personal. From the outset, nothing appeared random.

The case can be made murder was the ultimate goal when considering the fact James Baker was meant to hold the gun on the couple while Alvin Tyler took the money. Baker lost his nerve and pleaded to forget the entire episode. Tyler took the gun and murdered John without a single request for the money known to be possessed by the man. The victim supposedly carried nearly two hundred dollars; a lot of money in 1936. In reality he carried over twenty-seven hundred dollars. Looking at the situation rationally, that amount alone would have paid for half a house during the days of the Depression. That may have rendered moot the need to continue committing crimes for profit. Except for those possessed by a criminal bent.

Margaret Slater is a true-life family member, and Baby's sister-in-law. She did in fact work for the FBI and was transferred to the IRS when the FBI moved the management of the office to Miami in 1937.

Oddities continued surrounding this case when I learned it was a mere two days after Clyde Hysler received the death penalty for the murder of Mayme Surrency that Alvin Tyler and James Baker escaped from the local jail. With the aid of an outsider offering a hacksaw blade, seventeen young men escaped that night. Baker was recaptured hours later. The two most violent prisoners, one being Alvin Tyler, were never re-apprehended. Fortuitous for the FBI, there was a prisoner on federal charges who was one of the 17. His name was Loman Rivers, and his escape allowed the FBI to control the search effort. How odd it was that seventeen men escaped a downtown jail, and the two most violent were never heard from again. Seventeen inmates roaming the streets of Jacksonville offered a great deal of confusion. This provided a plausible redirection of search efforts toward those less violent, and away from Alvin Tyler. Another valid assumption.

My wife's grandfather, Noble Enge, was killed on July 24, 1938. His body was found by his wife, Miriam, in the family's chicken coop. He had, earlier in his life, run for county commission, as had his brother Axle. The reprint of the cartoon from the Florida Metropolis from 1915 is genuine. Tangible evidence the family I married into were genuinely good humans, who wished for a level playing field for all of humanity to compete.

Mayme's brother Senator John Swearingen was killed on a lonely road outside Bartow, Florida in 1931. In 1898, at the age of twenty, John did fight in the Immune regiments in Cuba during the Spanish American war. Around the time of John's death, Santo Trafficante and Ignacio Antinori did indeed combine forces to spread bolita throughout the state.

Mayme did have an addiction to Laudanum and other drugs of the day as a result of a hysterectomy. This was in the early 1900s while the family lived in Bartow, and she did sell a lot of the family's assets to feed her addiction. Her actions precipitated the family's move to Jacksonville.

John B. Hysler, Clyde Hysler's uncle, was murdered by federal agents on the Saint Johns River Bridge on September 26, 1937. Again, such an odd occurrence for the man known as the Liquor King. Why the heavy-handed justice for a bootlegger? Maybe he was about to expose the family's connection to not only mobsters like Al Capone, but to a criminal element within the FBI? Was he about to expose something that needed silencing? More valid questions.

The United States Supreme Court did hear the arguments of Clyde Hysler five days after Pearl Harbor. The conviction was upheld. Hysler and James Baker were put to death at Raiford on June 15, 1942.

When creating fiction from fact, we sometimes lose sight of important figures whose contribution to the story actually made the tale worth telling. Sheriff Rex Sweat and his deputies worked tirelessly to bring the three men to justice. John Harrel was the prosecutor of the day who did his best to ensure an eye-for-an-eye was the penalty levied against evil. I'm certain these men's souls are aware of our appreciation.

Some may be asking themselves, "which family member is Louis related to?" Carol Enge (two-year-old at the beginning of our story), Goldman Scott is my most wonderful mother-in-law. I wouldn't trade her for all the tea in China. If not for this wonderful woman, I would not have my wife in my life.

Please share the story of John and Mayme with family and friends. Their presence has been lost far too long. Less than fourteen years from the writing of this fictional story will be the one hundredth anniversary of the occurrence of John and Mayme's murder. It is imperative each family embrace the experiences of generations lost. For that is the foundation of our humanity.